The Heart of Addisen

Belle A. DeCosta

For my daughter Jeannie and grandson Ian.
My center, and my sun.

All my love.

"Life is a series of commas, not periods."
—*Matthew McConaughey*

Acknowledgments

Thank you to my editor, Martha Reynolds, for your skill, insight, encouragement, advice, and guidance on my writing journey. You are a treasure, and I so appreciate you.

Thank you to Steven and Dawn Porter of Stillwater River Publications and the founders of the Association of Rhode Island Authors (ARIA). You and your talented staff, notably Matthew St. Jean for his beautiful and intuitive cover art, allow me the joy of writing minus the headaches of publishing and distribution. And ARIA (now over 300 members) gives local authors a platform, voice, and opportunities we would not otherwise be awarded. Both are priceless.

Thank you to my friends and family for understanding the unanswered phone calls and broken plans when my creative juices flow and I disappear into my story. I am blessed to have you in my life.

Thank you to my young hound Trista, who refuses to lift her head from my keyboard until we break for exercise and fresh air, even when I don't think I need it. Which, of course, I always do.

And I'm most grateful to you, my readers. With the volumes of books available, I am honored you chose to sit with my story. Enjoy!

The Heart of Addisen

Chapter I

Caroline poured the day's first mug of coffee, rubbed the sleep from her eyes, and headed out to the deck. She stretched out on a chaise and tucked an afghan around her, more for comfort than to ward off the chill. Her mother, God rest her soul, had knitted and crocheted a mountain of shawls and throws throughout the years, and Caroline always felt her mom's warmth and presence when enfolded in one.

Swaddled in her mother's hug, she inhaled the enticing scent of fresh coffee mingled with pine and settled into her favorite part of the day: dawn. She never tired of watching the sunrise. The sky awakened from black to violet, indigo, and deep red, fading to orange, blue, and yellow as it fully woke. The colors shone on the lake as if it were a mirror, reflecting the magnificence of it all back to the heavens. A self-deprecating smile crossed Caroline's lips at the thought. Dawn hadn't always been a thing of beauty for her. A few short years ago, daybreak marked the end of an all-nighter spent placating her vices of tequila and emotionless sex to avoid facing her inner turmoil. It meant standing under the sleet of an icy shower, downing a handful of ibuprofen with a pot of coffee, then emptying the contents of stomach into the toilet on her way out the door to work. Dawn represented a bitter ending to the previous ugly twenty-hours rather than the beginning of a fresh, new day.

But that was then, and this was now. Since moving from Manhattan to Addisen, Maine, daybreak had become a time for quiet contemplation and counting her blessings. *So many things to be grateful for,* she thought. The move happened because she had discovered her mother's journal four years ago, which provided much-needed guidance at a pivotal time in her life. Its counsel led her to develop the trusted friendship she now cherished with Emmy and, finally, with herself. Both were a long time coming but worth the wait. Caroline's heart warmed at the thought of Emmy; she was Otis's cousin, and Caroline's first true friend. A friendship forged during Caroline's early days in Addisen had grown into a sisterhood. The diary's teachings introduced her to nature and its ability to heal and to fully appreciate the spirituality it inspires. A spirituality she now embraced at her core. As if on cue, a cardinal touched down. "Good morning, Mom," Caroline whispered. The bird studied her face and, satisfied all was well, cocked its head and flew off to start the day.

Then there was Otis, her soulmate, the real deal. When they met, Caroline was convinced love was unattainable to her, and the attraction she felt for him was purely physical. *Boy, was I ever wrong!* The thought made her grin. Their passion continued to grow with time, but it was their surreal connection that deepened their bond. Not that they didn't butt heads from time to time—they were both stubborn and had strong personalities. But it always came back to the fact they needed each other to breathe. It was that simple.

And out of that oneness, the ultimate blessing of all was conceived: Teddy. Theodore William Addisen, to be precise. Named after Otis's maternal grandfather and Caroline's deceased father, he would eventually inherit Addisen. The lake

and surrounding forest had been in Otis's family for generations, each one leaving their mark on the legacy. The result
is a piece of Americana tucked into a pristine setting. Teddy
would learn of his ancestry and develop the inevitable pride
in Addisen as he grew older. But for now, his only concerns
are pancakes for breakfast, walks in the woods with Mom,
fishing with Dad, and Charlie by his side. Charlie, their golden
retriever and Addisen's honorary mayor, is Teddy's constant
companion. From the minute he laid eyes on the baby, the
dog took on the role of nanny. He only leaves Teddy's side to
get Otis or Caroline to tend to his young master's needs. The
devotion is mutual and a thing of beauty to witness.

Moreover, both parents are eternally grateful for Charlie's
boundless energy and the continuous entertainment he provides for their young son. With a head full of light brown
curls, an infectious grin, and dark eyes, Teddy is the spitting
image of Otis. His temperament, however, is all Caroline.
With his insatiable curiosity and fearlessness, he is a spitfire
in perpetual motion. Caroline wouldn't have it any other way.
She loves how he explores everything, pushes boundaries to
see how far they stretch, marvels at the simplest things, and
soaks up all he learns like a sponge. Yes, he is a handful, but
he enjoys every minute of the day until his little body wears
out and reluctantly gives in to sleep.

Warmed with thoughts of her son and enjoying the colorful sky painted by the first light of day, Caroline felt her
husband's presence before his touch. Otis whispered, "Good
morning, milady," and gently moved her long auburn curls
to kiss the back of her neck, running his hand inside her top
to cup her breast. A small moan escaped as she reminded him
Teddy would be up soon. He slid underneath her and rolled
her over on top of him. "No worries. I just checked, and he's
still snoring. And I promised Charlie an extra slice of breakfast bacon if he gave us a heads up, should that change."

"So why are we still wearing clothes?" she purred.

Staring provocatively into her eyes, he sat her up to straddle him and slowly unbuttoned her top. "My thoughts exactly" were the last words spoken.

Afterward, lying sated, sandwiched between the warmth of her man's body and the sun's first rays, Caroline lolled in the magical place their lovemaking always took her. A place where dreams intermingled with reality and encased her in a fog of complete bliss. *Yes, life was good. Very good.*

Chapter II

Otis and Caroline's afterglow abruptly ended when Charlie let out a joyous bark, signaling their son Teddy's start to the day. They scrambled to put their clothes on in the time it took a whirlwind of fur and footy pajamas to barrel down the stairs. Caroline pulled a tee-shirt over her head as a chorus of barking and "Mommy, Daddy, Mommy, Daddy, me and Charlie opened our eyes!" sounded through the living room and onto the deck. She turned just in time to catch her son as he threw himself into her arms. She was struck by her overwhelming love for this little being as she held him close and kissed him into a fit of giggles.

"Good morning, my little prince."

"Good morning, Mommy," he said, wiggling to get down. Teddy raced to his dad, who lifted him over his head. A raspberry on his belly and a kiss on his forehead was the price he paid to be freed.

"Morning, Bear, ready to conquer the day?" Otis asked.

"Yep. Daddy, where's your shirt?"

"Mommy's wearing it."

Caroline looked down. *Oh crap, I am.* She looked back up at her husband, who was grinning ear to ear.

"Mommy, how come you have Daddy's shirt?"

"Yeah, Mom, how come?" Otis asked innocently.

Caroline was ready. "Because I found it lying on the deck and wanted to help Daddy by picking it up."

Caroline hadn't survived at the top of Manhattan's advertising world for years by floundering when caught off guard.

Otis, amused, shot his wife an admiring look, and mouthed the word *Touché* over Teddy's head. Caroline's voiceless, *you will pay,* was accompanied by a sassy smirk and a wink. Otis had no doubt he would.

The boy squirmed out of his father's arms and took off for the kitchen. "Daddy, I want pancakes!" When no one followed, he turned back to see both parents with feet firmly planted, arms crossed. Realizing his mistake, he ran back. "Please, I want pancakes. I meant, please." Otis ruffled his curls. "Much better. Pancakes you shall have, Bear."

The family was finishing breakfast when Otis's cousin Emmy came in, carrying her son Caleb. Caleb, four months younger than Teddy, was just as curious and energetic but in a more thoughtful way. Teddy plowed ahead, devil be damned, while Caleb seemed to assess the situation first. *Just like their moms,* Caroline thought. Even at their young age, it was obvious how close the second cousins were.

Emmy and Caroline had forged a friendship over five years ago, the summer Caroline was forced to take a hiatus from her NYC life. The advertising firm Perkins, Gavin, and Gavin ordered her to take the summer and regain her footing or lose her job. When her beloved brother Will agreed she was breaking down, he convinced her to spend time at the old family cabin in Maine. Caroline went kicking and screaming but knew now it was what saved her—from herself, as well as a fatal fall off the precipitous cliff she was unknowingly dangling from.

Emmy's "Helloooo" pulled Caroline out of her reverie.

"Sorry, what did I miss?"

"I was asking if the Morrises had approved the designs yet?"

"No, they want to go over them one more time. We have a Zoom meeting at 11:00."

On top of being best friends and relatives, the women were business partners. Emmy had a passion for gardening and a gifted eye for design. She'd always wanted to start a business but lacked the funds. Upon leaving the advertising world, Caroline needed a project to sate her endless ambition and had money to invest. In a few short years, Emmy's creativity and knowledge of horticulture, combined with Caroline's keen business sense and marketing ability had made Cardinal Garden Design a success. Already well-known and respected in Maine, New Hampshire, and Vermont, the Morris account would be their first in the Boston area and a big step towards opening the lucrative market the city's upscale suburbs offered. Emmy's dream of Cardinal being supplied by its own nursery could become a reality sooner rather than later.

Their conversation was interrupted by the ring of an old-fashioned bicycle bell and squeals of delight from the boys. "Dolcie's here!"

Dolcie, previously known as Dolores, was hired as the boys' nanny but quickly became a surrogate grandmother. With Emmy's mom living in Florida and her husband Dan's, Caroline's, and Otis's mothers deceased, Dolcie filled a void in all their lives. She and her husband Bert, an avid fisherman and hunter, had owned a cabin on the lake for years and spent many enjoyable weekends there. But when they retired and moved to Addisen permanently, Dolores found it challenging to fill her days. Hearing the Addisens and Preaces needed a nanny, she was determined to be the first and last person to interview for the position; she was. When Caroline and Emmy asked for her credentials, she simply stated, "I raised five boys, and none of them ever disrespected us or went to jail." That was testament enough for the new moms. Slight in stature, she possessed a no-nonsense attitude and boundless energy. Her hair, the color of snow, was cut in a short bob and her crystal blue eyes missed nothing. Perfect for tending to two rambunctious boys. She scolded when needed, hugged in abundance, and always had a story. Teddy loved to hear how she got her name and asked her to tell the story often.

"Well, young man, one day, when you were just learning to say a few words, you toddled over to sit on my lap. I gave you a king-sized hug, and while you giggled, I pointed to me, saying, "Dolores loves Teddy," and pointed to you. You pointed to yourself, then to me, and clear as can be said, "Teddy—Dolcie," and grinned. "Been Dolcie ever since and proud of it."

She entered the kitchen with a preschooler hanging onto each leg, good-naturedly complaining. "I swear, you boys get heavier every day. It's like dragging two sacks of potatoes around." Teddy and Caleb collapsed in laughter as Dolcie reached down and gave each one a tickle. "Now give your moms a kiss and hug so they can go to work." They happily obliged, and the trio headed outside to a chorus of, "Dolcie, can we do this first? Let's play this now."

"She is a godsend," Emmy said.

"And then some," Caroline added.

It was a gorgeous day, so they decided to take the skiff to work. Cardinal Garden Design was based across the lake in what used to be Caroline's parents' cabin, although they were starting to outgrow the space. "If we open up the Boston area, we'll have to move for sure," Emmy pointed out as they docked the skiff.

"You mean *when* we open it up. And we'll deal with

more elbow room when that happens," Caroline stated. "In the meantime, let's close the Morris deal and get this party started!"

"How about we start with a small get-together first?" Emmy quipped. "I'm worried about expanding too rapidly."

"Baby steps," the friends chorused with a smile. Caroline's mom had used that phrase countless times to try to instill an even pace and patience in her charge-like-a-bull daughter. Unfortunately, it took Caroline well into adulthood and a transformation to finally heed the message. She now repeated it to herself so often it had become her mantra.

Emmy admired her friend's confidence and assertiveness but was determined to be the calming force whose voice kept Caroline grounded. Well, as much as anyone could anchor her. Caroline had mellowed in the last four years, but the underlying current to move ahead fast still flowed in her veins. Was this its opportunity to become white water rapids again, washing away all else? Only time would tell.

Chapter III

Otis started his truck and whistled for Charlie. Attached as the dog was to Teddy, he was Otis's right-hand man and enjoyed the job. Charlie came running and hopped in the cab, tail wagging. "Time to get to work and prepare for the season, boy." Otis was rewarded with a slobbery kiss, and the team began their rounds. He loved this time of year in Addisen, his land coming to life after a long winter, much like himself. Sure, both had a pulse through the dormant months, but Otis's spirit lay in hibernation, much like nature's, until the thaw.

Like his ancestors before him, he oversaw all operations and, with the help of a competent team of managers, kept Addisen Lake a coveted destination. Still, Otis preferred to do much of the repairs and upkeep himself. He reveled in caring for the property, much like a parent raising a child. It was his blood and responsibility to nurture until he passed it to the next in line.

Through the generations, Addisen men had taken miles of wilderness and an overgrown lake (won in a poker game) and built an oasis for sportsmen and families alike. There were trails for avid hikers and paths for the faint of heart. The small town, reminiscent of a past era, consisted of a general store owned by Emmy's husband, Dan, a laundromat, a gas station, and a barbershop. Perched around the large lake were a summer camp for kids, rental cabins, campgrounds, and cabins owned by weekend fishermen and families. For his contribution, Otis had stocked the lake with fish and added a rental shack with canoes, fishing boats, jet skis, and tubes.

Ankle deep in mud, Otis was in his element, assessing what had to be done before Memorial Day. Some of the rental cabins needed new roofs, the campground had to be cleared of winter debris, and a couple of floorboards needed replacing in a bunkhouse or two. Stopping at each amenity, they would peruse the area, Otis taking notes while Charlie checked for unwanted critters. They continued and found a tree down on the south end dirt road, blocking access to the family cabins. "We'll need to take care of that ASAP, Charlie. People will arrive soon to check how their cabins faired in the winter." The dog put his front paws on the massive trunk as if to roll it out of the way. Otis chuckled and patted his head. "I think it's gonna take a little more than that, fella. But thanks for trying."

They circled back the other way to complete the day's look-over and hit huge potholes on the other side of the tree. Otis surmised the tree had blocked runoff from the thaw and rain, washing away the dirt. He made a mental note to call Dan and borrow his backhoe. "Well, Charlie, the first order of business is that tree and filling in the craters. Agreed?" The dog barked his assent, and they headed home, the preliminary inspection finished. By that time, master, dog, and truck were mud-caked, top to bottom, and needed hosing down.

Dolcie saw them coming and stopped them mid-climb on the deck stairs. "Don't even think about it," she scolded. She handed Otis a robe, towels, soap, and dog shampoo.

"March yourself and your beast to the outdoor shower."

"Outdoor shower! Do you know how cold it is out here now the sun's sinking low?" Otis whined.

"You want to play in the mud, you pay the price. Now go, shoo. It's not getting any warmer."

"For Chrissake, we were working, not playing."

Dolcie shrugged. "Mud is mud."

Otis turned and headed back down the stairs, Charlie at his heels. Didn't matter who you were or how old; you didn't mess with Dolcie.

★ ★ ★

The Morris call was a success, and Cardinal Garden Design had a new market to pursue. Caroline's wheels were already spinning. "There's so much to think about. An urban marketing strategy, pricing, staff for the area, and more office space here. And your nursery, Emmy." The look on Emmy's face stopped her short. "I'm doing it again, aren't I? Too much, too fast." She took a deep breath and exhaled slowly. "I can't help it—it's my mind's default setting."

"I know," Emmy said. "But remember the work/life balance promise you made to yourself when we first started? I know it's a struggle for you, and the more successful we get, the harder it will be. But you owe it to yourself and your family to keep it in check."

Caroline recalled a pivotal moment that could have ended abominably during her brief return to NYC. A cardinal saved her, standing on the balcony railing with one foot tucked in its feathers. *Balance.* "You're right. And I have just the cure to stop the madness." She gave her friend a thumbs up and headed out the door.

"Have a great walk," Emmy said with a smile.

Through her mother's journaled words and visits as a

cardinal, Caroline learned that connecting as one with the spirituality of the earth and all her treasures brought tranquility that encased her soul. It always, without fail, centered her and had brought Caroline through a self-destructive time, to the place she embodied now.

Caroline stepped outside, closed her eyes, and turned her face to the sun. Breathing deeply, she inhaled the mixed scent of pine, damp earth, and lake, letting it replace the stale smell of an indoor space closed against the chill. She started up her favorite trail, taking in all she loved about Addisen's springs. The mornings were still cold but held the promise of warm afternoons like this. The pines, always a burst of color amidst the brown and white of winter, seemed a deeper shade of green. The buds were starting to appear on trees and shrubs, like tiny heads popping up after a long nap. The lake, slate gray in the winter, was starting to soak up the warmer sunlight and occasionally sparkle, a dress rehearsal for summer. She watched critters scurry and birds flutter, all busy preparing nests for their impending babies. Spring. A season of birth, but also rebirth. Proof that dormant doesn't mean dead. That all things are relative to how you see them. "And therein lies my day's lesson," Caroline said out loud. Her cardinal touched down on a young sapling just ahead, as if on cue. "Thanks, Mom, " she whispered as the bird took flight.

With her mind safely restored to a state of rationalization, Caroline returned to the office to discuss the next step with Emmy. The women, so engrossed in outlining the immediate needs of phase one, lost track of time until Emmy's husband, Dan, walked in. "Do you two plan to come home tonight?" he teased. Ignoring the remark, Emmy jumped up, threw herself into his arms, and started dancing him around the office.

"We got the Morris account! The Cardinal has landed in Boston!"

"That's awesome," he said, picking her up and spinning her around. "But I always knew you would."

"That makes two of us," Caroline said, beaming.

The three of them chatted briefly, then locked up to head home. Stepping outside, they noticed the chill and rapidly fading light. Dan insisted the two ladies take his truck home, and he would cross the lake in the skiff. This protective chivalry, naturally present in men like Dan and Otis, still touched Caroline, even after four years. Having lived in the 'everyone for themselves' concrete jungle of corporate Manhattan, it was initially an anomaly, not to be trusted. Now she fully appreciated the instinct, born in a man's heart, to care for those he loved above himself. *Correction: a real man,* she thought. Caroline smiled and urged Emmy to start the truck. She was suddenly in a hurry to get home.

Chapter IV

Caroline was met at the door by a wet dog, a chocolate-covered son, and a sulking husband. Sensing that this was no time to laugh, Emmy quickly grabbed a sticky Caleb and headed out the door with a wave.

"What in the world..." Otis held up a hand to stop Caroline, and his accompanying look did the trick. She stripped her son down and put him in the farmer's sink while Otis grabbed a towel and baby shampoo upstairs. When Caroline asked Teddy what happened, like his father, he was quiet as a mouse.

"Sweetie, why won't you tell Mommy? Are you afraid you'll get in trouble?" Teddy shook his head no.

"Then what is it?"

The little one began to cry. "I don't want Daddy to get in trouble again."

"Again?"

"Dolcie already scolded him two times."

Stifling a chortle, she said, "No worries, sweetie. Mommy will ask Daddy about it later." *Oh, I so cannot wait to hear this story.* Happy to be off the tattletale hook, Teddy babbled on about the cookies and finger paintings they'd made earlier with Dolcie and asked if he could have macaroni and cheese for supper and a cookie for dessert? "You bet, little man. Then off to bed with you and Charlie, no grumbling. Deal?"

"Deal," he promised.

As his wife tended to and fed Teddy, Otis set about drying Charlie, no easy task with a 120-lb. golden retriever. They finished about the same time, and a still mute Otis started to make dinner while Caroline tucked Teddy in and read him a story.

Finally, they sat down to dinner, and Caroline raised her eyebrows in question. Otis filled her in. He told her about coming home beaten and dirty, but happy, with a fire in his belly. "You know how I love poking around, finding the first list of fixes needed for a new season." Caroline took a bite and nodded. Otis told her how Dolcie forbade him to enter the house, *his* house, before showering outdoors. His mood soured; he obliged and stewed throughout the shower. When he and Charlie, mud free and freezing, raced through the back door, Dolcie stopped them again and ordered Charlie outside until dry.

Seeing Teddy and Caleb take it all in, Otis felt the need to man up and told her no way. She scolded him again. "Something about the smell of wet dog in the carpets, and she opened the door to put Charlie out. I closed the door and said, 'My dog, my house,' which set her off, some." 'Well,' she said, 'that it is. I'll take my leave for the day since you have all the answers. I'll see you tomorrow.' She grabbed her coat and was gone." Otis continued.

"Seeing red, I told the boys to sit tight and ran upstairs to grab the dryer for Charlie. I swear I wasn't gone ten seconds, but I came down to two chocolate-covered kids. I guess the three of them were set to make chocolate milk when I first came in. After Dolcie left and knowing I had to dry the dog, they took matters into their own hands. That's the exact moment you arrived on the scene," he finished.

Caroline doubled over in laughter, much to her husband's chagrin. "It's not funny," he said, annoyed.

"Oh, yes, it is," she managed through fits of giggles. Once Caroline regained control, she wiped her eyes and recapped the story as she saw it.

"The two adults threw a temper tantrum and stormed out of the room, leaving a pair of four-year-olds to do the grownup thing and complete a task, which went about as well as expected. I think it's hilarious."

Otis gave a sheepish grin. "Put that way, I see the humor. But still, Dolcie crossed a line. I'll discuss it tomorrow with her."

Caroline took her man's hand and led him towards the stairs. "Come on, lord of the manor, I have a great idea on how you can exert your manhood."

She might never fully understand a man's ego, but she certainly knew how to restore it.

★   ★   ★

After their lovemaking, Otis was spooned behind her, snoring softly while Caroline lay wide awake. Sex had always energized her, made her feel alive and raring to go. She often wondered if it had the same effect on other women. On the other hand, men drifted off to la-la land like sedated tigers. At times like this, she envied them. She gently disengaged herself from her husband's embrace, grabbed her robe, tiptoed to the hallway, and quietly closed the door. After she checked on Teddy and Charlie, who were also snoring, Caroline went to the reading room to write in her journal.

Their reading room was much too casual to be called a library, yet two of its walls had floor-to-ceiling bookshelves filled mostly with inherited books. (Both of Caroline's parents, as well as Otis's mother, had been avid readers). White walls and shelves, and huge windows overlooking the lake, created a light and airy atmosphere. Blue flowered, chintz-covered chairs and love seats, accented with bohemian scatter rugs and her mom's crocheted pieces, gave it a feel of Nantucket chic.

Initially, Otis's father had kept his deceased wife's bookshelves in the bedroom to keep her nearby. She had died of an aneurysm shortly after giving birth to Otis, and his dad had never loved another. "I've got my boy, my land, and the memory of the love of my life. That's all I need," he would say. Upon retiring to Florida, he took only her favorite texts. When Otis moved into the master suite, he left the rest where they were, feeling connected to his mom through her books. However, once Caroline moved in, having her memory in their boudoir seemed disrespectful, not to mention awkward. Otis converted one of the guest rooms into a 'library' and created a space full of their parents' presence and memories. Caroline's mom's rocker, which had brought her so much comfort through her dark days, held a place of honor next to the only piece of dark wood in the room: the end table from her childhood, besieged with water rings, gouges, and scratches, layered with years of polish and fingerprints. Caroline cherished it for all the memories it held.

As was her habit before she journaled, Caroline sat in the rocker, wrapped herself in the worn afghan draped over its back (her mom's favorite), and patted the tabletop a couple of times, as you would a beloved pet's head. Feeling her mom now with her, she began her entry. Caroline didn't write every day but deemed today's events noteworthy. She recorded the feeling of nailing the Morris account and how she instantly reverted to her old mindset. She wrote what a gift Emmy was, always there to reel her in and set her back on course. How nature's handholding and whispers led her back to center, as it always did. She reiterated the comedy skit that she arrived home to and the lesson learned by Otis and, hopefully, eventually, Dolcie. Finally, Caroline tried to articulate the feeling that overcame her every time she took stock of her blessed life. Her mother had written so eloquently, her words real and expressive, putting Caroline into the moment and her heart, imparting life's lessons without intention. Her daughter was determined to provide the same for her children in her own journal. Still not ready for sleep, Caroline read some of her earliest entries from five years ago.

I think about the wreath I made for our front door a while back. Dried speedwell encompasses the inner circle, their blue blossoms representing the lake. I added a nest to portray our home woven with a red ribbon to acknowledge the cardinals, our family members, who surround us with protection and love. And I collected nature's treasures from the lake's different amenities to honor each generation's contribution to the family legacy.

This morning I tucked an egg into the nest, my way of sharing the joyous, if unexpected, news with Otis. Tonight, after we watch the sunset, I will stop at the door, reach behind me for his hand, place it on my abdomen, and gently touch the egg.

My plan worked beautifully. He stood perfectly still for an eternal moment before I heard a sob, and his hands turned me to face him. I stared into my man's eyes and was struck by his expression of pure, unadulterated joy. We were both rendered speechless; Otis by the news, me by his reaction. He leaned in and gifted me the most perfect kiss. Soft, tender, almost awestruck. So full of protective, gentle love. He laid his forehead against mine and whispered, "We created a life." Our connection rose to a new level as we shared the wonder of it all. Overwhelmed, the dam broke, and we laughed, cried, danced around, and high-fived.

And now there are three…

I can't rest. I'm a mess. It's been a couple of weeks since I broke the news to Otis, and while his feet remain off the ground, mine seem to have landed in hormonal muck. Mired in a swamp of apprehension, excitement, fear, anticipation, insecurity, confidence, panic, elation, and worry. Torn between I've got this, and what ifs. A short time ago, I couldn't take care of myself, much less another human being. Am I ready for this? A little late for that question now. God, I can't screw this up. A baby. A. Baby. Am I nurturing enough? I have plenty of energy, but what about patience? I'm not known for an overabundance of tolerance. Can I learn? Will this be different? UGH! Mom, I need your counsel. What would you do? And suddenly, I have the answer. She would've talked to her best friend, Donna, of course. I will share the news with Emmy tomorrow, and she will help me work through it all. Mom comes to the rescue again.

Caroline smiled, remembering Emmy's reaction to the news. She squealed and hugged her so tight Caroline almost lost her breath. Over the moon, she babbled on for a minute before she noticed the look on her friend's face and stopped short. "What's wrong, sweetie?" Emmy asked. Caroline broke down in tears, ramping up her friend's concern. "Is it a high-risk pregnancy? Are you not well?" Caroline could only shake her head no. Emmy put both hands on her shoulders and gave a squeeze. "Caroline, look at me. What is it?"

"What if I screw it all up?" Caroline sobbed.

Emmy had let out a sigh of relief, handed the mother-to-be a handful of tissues, and stated, "You won't."

"How do you know?"

"Because it's not your way. You thrive in a challenge; it's how you roll. And parenthood is the ultimate project to conquer. No, you will shine as a mother. Besides, you're not in this alone. Remember Otis?"

The simplicity of her words, said with such conviction, was precisely what Caroline needed. They pulled her out of the storm of fear and self-doubt that formed in her mind. She shifted from remembering what a mess she used to be to all she had successfully accomplished to turn herself around.

A friendship as connected as mine and Emmy's is a god-send, like having your own earth angel. With that thought, Caroline turned out the light, finally ready to do some snoring of her own.

Chapter V

Breakfast the following morning was lively since everyone tried to talk at once. Otis was excited about getting Addisen ready for a new season, Caroline was wound up about the Morris account and the potential it offered, and Teddy could barely sit still long enough to eat. Today was the big day. "Mom, can we go now, please?"

"Not until you've finished your pancakes."

"But I'm not hungry."

"Whoa, Bear, you can't hike all the way up the ridge on an empty stomach," his father said. Defeated, Teddy sighed and stuck a forkful of syrup-ladened pancakes into his mouth.

Caroline had taken Teddy on walks along the trail behind their house since his birth. She wanted him to grow up as one with nature's life around him, to appreciate the wooded wonder and all it holds. They had graduated from an infant wrap across her chest to a jogging stroller, to Teddy's toddling, then hitching a piggyback ride home. For the last year, her son insisted he could walk the entire time, even though she could see his little legs tire. When Caroline suggested they shorten the walk, Teddy, highly insulted, started to go a little farther each day. *Like mother like son,* Caroline thought with pride. *So determined and driven,* she seasoned with a dash of worry.

She teased him one day about wanting to walk around the world. He stopped and pointed to a small ridge in the near distance. "No, Mommy, just to up there."

"But why?" she asked.

"To see everything from the top."

Yep, he's my blood, for sure, she thought. "Alright then, you've set a goal. Let's keep training."

Today was the day they were going all the way, and Teddy couldn't wait any longer. He shoveled the pancakes down as fast as he could chew and looked at his mother with pleading eyes. "Okay, okay," she said good-naturedly. "Let's get you dressed and climb that ridge."

Otis helped Teddy put a bottle of water and a snack bar in his little backpack, reminding him smart hikers paced themselves. "Got it, Daddy," he yelled as he ran out the door, hollering for his mother to hurry. With a wink, Caroline kissed her husband and asked him to send out a search and rescue team if they weren't back in an hour or so.

Once on the trail, Teddy slowed down to find all his forest friends. He searched the trees for birds he heard chirping and walked softly, hoping bunnies and chipmunks would come out to say hi. As was their ritual, mother and son closed their eyes and took a couple of deep breaths, allowing the mixed scent of the forest and new growth to fill their lungs and infuse with their bloodstream. Of course, Teddy was too young to realize this was happening; he just knew it made him feel good. After a short time, the pair thanked Gaia (Mother Earth) and God for the beauty and life inhabiting their surroundings and continued their trek.

Caroline had an old mail sack strapped over her shoulder to carry any treasures they found along the way. She and Emmy made personalized and all-occasion wreaths and sold them through Cardinal Design. What started as a hobby between friends had become a lucrative part of the business. Teddy loved to help by hunting down various feathers and different-sized pinecones. Not long into the walk, Caroline stopped to cut wildflowers. When she no longer heard her son, she looked up and saw a most beautiful happening unfold.

Just to the right of the path, Teddy stood within six feet of a fawn. Both were instinctively still as if to assure the other they meant no harm. The two young babes stared in awe of one another, forming an almost visible bond, their innocence enabling a mutual trust that age would not have allowed. Teddy slowly reached out his hand that held the greens he'd collected, and the fawn tentatively moved forward to take them. After a nibble or two, she nuzzled Teddy's hand and walked back into the thicket.

Spellbound, Teddy remained rooted in place. Caroline quietly walked over to him, knelt beside him, took his still-outstretched hand, and kissed it. He turned to her, his face so alight with pure wonder and joy, she got dewy-eyed. "Wow," he whispered.

"Wow, indeed," Caroline replied.

Emotional, Teddy hugged his mom's neck tight and said, "Hey, let's get going," breaking the spell but not the moment's magic. The feelings invoked by the beauty of that ethereal encounter would be a lifelong gift for the young boy and his mother, too.

Getting back to the mission, the two made their way up the gradual incline, searching for forest gems while Teddy chattered on endlessly about everything, something he did when excited. Caroline observed that his enthusiasm was way over the top between the fawn and conquering the ridge, and she loved every minute of it. In the middle of a story about Charlie, Teddy abruptly turned to his mother and asked, "Where was her mommy?"

It was a question Caroline had been asking herself. She gave the answer she hoped was true. "Watching, hidden by the trees." *Please don't be a victim of the highway.*

"Why didn't she come out?"

"Because she didn't want to scare you. Like I didn't want to frighten the fawn. So, both mommas stayed out of sight to let their babies make friends."

"I am not a baby. I'm almost five," Teddy informed her.

"You're right; I stand corrected," she soothed. *I don't care if you're a hundred and five; you will always be my baby,* she thought to pacify herself.

They reached the top of the ridge, and Caroline had to grab the hood of Teddy's sweatshirt to stop him from racing to the edge. Carefully, she walked them to a spot where they could safely see the world from the top, as Teddy had wished. For a second time that morning, Teddy was awestruck. "Wow. Is this how the birds feel when they fly, Mom?"

"Pretty much, sweetie."

"If I were a bird, I'd fly all the time."

"You would need to land to eat and build a nest for your family."

"Yeah, I guess. But this is so cool."

The metaphor was not lost on Caroline. *Yes it is, my little man. But so is nesting.* Still, part of her missed challenging her wingspan to fly higher occasionally.

"I want to sit on the edge and dangle my feet in the air." *Of. Course. You. Do.*

"No. It's too dangerous. When you're older, you can."

"Like tomorrow?"

Caroline laughed. "Why are you always in a hurry to grow up?"

"'Cause grownups get to do everything they want."

"No one ever gets to do everything they want. Sometimes you need to compromise to be complete."

"Huh?"

"Give up some of one thing to get another to be fully happy."

"Well, you still get to do more than us kids."

Unable to argue that point, she quietly took in the view, letting her son savor his top-of-the-world moment. Eventually, she suggested they head home and share the morning's adventures with Caleb and Dolcie. Eager to tell his tales, Teddy took off at a run. "Race ya, Mom."

Yep, he's my son.

Chapter VI

Teddy barreled through the door, almost knocking Dolcie over in his excitement to share his adventures. "Some wild beast chasing you, little man?" Dolcie asked.

"No, but I made a new friend. A baby deer kissed my hand, and her mom let her and everything, It was so cool! And then Mom and me climbed to the sky and sat on top of the world and felt like birds do when they fly."

Dolcie raised an eyebrow at Caroline. She wasn't one for filling young heads with fantasies or inflating experiences with overactive imaginations.

"All true stories," Caroline confirmed as Teddy ran to find Caleb. "Dolcie, he's not even five years old; to him, that small climb was to the top of the world."

"And the fawn's mother? She let humans get that close to her young? This is the forest, not a petting zoo. Chances are—"

Caroline cut her off. "She wasn't undernourished or timid as an orphan would be. I believe her mother was as captivated as I by the beautiful interaction between our young and allowed it to play out."

Dolcie rolled her eyes. "If you say so." A pragmatist, she didn't possess or understand Caroline's reverent connection to nature.

Caroline was already late for work but needed to address the incident between Otis and Dolcie as promised. Dolcie stopped her with a slight wave. "I realize I overstepped my bounds and have already apologized to him." With that settled, Caroline found the boys for a kiss goodbye and headed to work.

On the ride over, Caroline tried, unsuccessfully, to stop her mind from getting too far into the business's future. But she knew it would take less time for growth in Boston and surrounding suburbs than the rural areas and smaller cities of Cardinal's first four years. Emmy might think she should slow down, but Caroline knew the pace would pick up quickly and intended to be prepared. She decided, *I'll keep the planning to myself and share it in increments so Emmy doesn't get spook*ed. Caroline wasn't afraid of becoming obsessed now that she had the emotional tools and insight to stay centered. But truth be told, as much as she adored her family and life in Addisen, feelings of restlessness had crept in lately. Until now, she hadn't realized how much she had missed the anticipation of going after a monumental goal and making it happen.

Caroline allowed herself the adrenaline rush that made her nerves tingle and ignited her brain. Now confident she could maintain control, she welcomed back her drive and ambition. There was her son, the love of a good man, and the spirit of nature to keep her grounded. She was sure it would all come together with Otis's support and her mom's guidance.

Caroline found Emmy bent over Morris's blueprints, finalizing what was needed before she placed the orders. "Someone's in a good mood," she said to her partner. Caroline recounted the morning wonders with Teddy but left out her private a-ha moment. *No need to worry her,* Caroline reasoned. As close as the women were, Caroline knew they were sometimes on different pages.

While Emmy phoned the nurseries, Caroline mulled over the options for a Boston crew. Until now, Cardinal always put their staff up in a local motel if needed, but Boston prices made that impractical; paying for travel time and mileage made more sense.

Next, she designed a brochure for mass mailing (email and snail mail) to follow up with phone calls. She smiled at how Caroline of the Manhattan advertising world would scoff at the antiquated method but knew the old-fashioned way was best for this service. Caroline didn't see it as moving too fast but striking while the iron was hot. *We've got to nail down opportunities before they slip away.*

At lunchtime, the partners filled one another in on their morning's progress and then turned the conversation to personal, as friends do. Caroline shared what happened between Dolcie and Otis, resulting in the chocolate-covered boys they'd come home to. Once Emmy got control of her giggle fit, she shared her tale of the previous evening. Dan took one look at Caleb and put him in the kitchen sink without a word, squirted whipped cream on his head, and placed a cherry on top. "There, now you look good enough to eat," he said, and kissed his son's face, chanting "Yum, yum," to Caleb's delight.

"You're kidding," Caroline said through tears of laughter. Emmy held up her phone with the picture she managed to snap before Dan started his Cookie Monster impression. "That should be your Christmas card this year!" Caroline roared. Emmy agreed, and the two women got back to work.

Caroline's meeting with the foreman went well. He assured her his crew would welcome the extra money and deal with the interim commute. Caroline, always impressed by Otis's cooperation and mutual respect with his managers, had vowed to create the same environment at Cardinal Garden Design. Consequently, employees felt part of a team, which showed in their work and willingness to be flexible.

Satisfied with her day's accomplishments, she decided to stop her mind from racing by going home. Nothing rooted her like time spent with her guys, small, tall, and four-legged alike. Caroline found all the above, running around outside playing tag. Getting out of the truck, she beeped the horn and was attacked by an army of love. Teddy raced into her arms at full tilt and held her as tightly as his little arms could. Otis walked toward her with that look in his eyes meant only for her and kissed her with purpose. Whining, Charlie danced circles around them until she bent down, and he could welcome her home with licks and paw shakes. "What a lucky lady I am," Caroline said with an ear-to-ear grin. "All this affection from three Prince Charmings just for me."

"Well-deserved, milady," Otis said, putting an arm around her shoulders. "Hey, who's up for make-your-own pizza night?"

"Yay! That's me and Charlie's favorite. Come on, boy, I'll make one 'specially for you," shouted Teddy as he barreled up the stairs. Delighted by their son's enthusiasm, Otis and Caroline followed close behind.

Otis fired up the grill, then rolled out the dough. Teddy made his usual sauce, cheese, more cheese, and cheese. For Charlie's pie, he spread peanut butter and topped it with liver dog treats and what little was left of the cheese. After dinner, Otis went up to bathe Teddy while Caroline cleaned up. She wasn't surprised to hear Teddy didn't make two pages of his bedtime story before he was sound asleep. He'd had quite the day.

Snuggled on the couch, sipping an espresso, Caroline tried to recreate the joy of witnessing their son's enchantment at the day's events for her husband. Otis had already heard the morning's happenings through excited Teddy's 4-year-old eyes. But to listen to his wife's account, through a fascinated parent's eye, completed the picture. Together, the two perspectives inspired emotions as if he was there. He kissed the top of her head and thanked her for the gift of inclusion. Once again, she melted at his heart. *Yes, I am one lucky lady and so blessed.*

Chapter VII

Caroline woke to the sound of rain. *No sunrise on the deck today* was her first thought. She rose quietly and slipped into sweatpants and a tee-shirt. She peeked in on her son and was awarded a tail thump from Charlie, letting her know all was well. After pouring a coffee, Caroline grabbed her journal and headed down to the lower level into a man cave that spanned the entire square footage of the house. Her heart softened as she took in the littlest man of the house additions to the décor. A coloring table sat in the office space next to his dad's desk, and a Spiderman blanket lay thrown over the leather recliner in front of the humungous TV. A train set wove throughout the room, and a ball pit now sat next to Otis's poker table. A miniature pinball machine nestled next to its pub-sized counterpart. It was the perfect space for father-son bonding. On a whim, wanting to feel them near, she took Otis's heavy sweatshirt off the hook and grabbed the Spiderman blanket.

Caroline let herself through the wall of folding glass doors that opened to a sitting area beneath the deck. She curled up on the porch swing Otis had moved from her parents' cabin and had hung from the deck flooring. Like the rocking chair, the swing held a special meaning for Caroline. It was a sacred spot for her. It's where she'd found comfort on many nights, working through her transition and coming to terms with her inner self. She had read passages from her mom's journal sitting in the very spot where most were written and gained insight into her mother as a woman, not just a mom. It was where she learned lessons as an adult, at her mother's knee from beyond. The wicker swing held many memories, thoughts, fears, and prayers of the McMerritt women. *Therein lies its magic and power of love,* Caroline believed.

Mother Nature offers so much to charm your consciousness and beguile your soul if you let her in. Warming her hands around the steaming mug, Caroline let the surrounding beauty tantalize her senses. She loved the smell of damp earth infused with traces of pine and lake water. She watched the rain hit the water, each drop creating circular ripples that reminded her of tiny ballet tutus. A coyote's howl echoed across the lake, harmonizing with an owl's hoot, while the rain kept a quiet, steady beat.

Her meditation now completed, Caroline gave thanks, reached for the journal, and began to write.

Good morning self. I have a confession, and you're the only one I can tell, for now, anyway. Yesterday, I experienced the rush of adrenaline I used to get going after a big account. It made me realize how much I've missed it—the challenge of landing a new client, the confidence in my ability to provide services that deliver desired results. I found it even more exhilarating because it was for our own company. I faced the feelings of restlessness that crept in here and there. I love my life and wouldn't trade it for anything, but is it fair to deny

myself such a core part of me? It's as if there are two sides to me; don't they both deserve to be nurtured?

I'm not the same Caroline of Manhattan. I have grown and flourished in the love of my son and husband, my beautiful Addisen. My drive and ambition have mellowed in the face of these gifts, but I now realize they remain an essential part of me. I believe both sides can co-exist peacefully and even benefit one another. But I'm apprehensive about how others will react. Will those closest to me trust me to stay centered?

Emmy gets nervous when I show the slightest bit of assertiveness or determination. Will she eventually see the benefits of a controlled, motivated, enterprising partner? And what of Otis? No, I needn't worry about him. Do I? He supports all I do and understands me better than I do myself. He will welcome back a toned-down version of the woman he initially fell for. Surely, he could never doubt my devotion to him, Teddy, and our little piece of heaven. It will all work out... baby steps...

Caroline sat a while longer in the cold, damp air, not minding it a bit. She welcomed it on her face. It turned her cheeks red and her hair got curlier by the minute. *Definitely a ponytail day,* she decided. Enfolded in Otis's sweatshirt, her hands tucked into Teddy's blanket, she was protected from any chill the weather, external or internal, threw at her. She brought the blanket up to her face and inhaled the faint scents of her men, chuckling at Charlie's ever-present dog hair. There was a time odors and hair would've disgusted her, not warmed her. *Yes, I've come a long, long way. How did I ever survive such*

an emotionally barren existence, she wondered. Her stomach growled, reminding her it was time for one of Otis's scrumptious weekend breakfasts, and she went in to join the family that now filled her reality's cup to the brim.

She found her crew in the kitchen, uncontrollably laughing over what Teddy called "an oops." He'd wanted chocolate chip pancakes and brought an open bag to the stove for his dad. Unaware Teddy was behind him, Otis was startled when he turned with a plate of bacon. Afraid of dropping the sizzling meat on his son, he swiveled back to the counter, sending the bacon flying in the opposite direction and knocking over a bowl of batter, which caused Teddy to spill the bag of chips. Charlie was already on cleanup, gobbling up the unexpected floor buffet. Gaining control, Otis looked at his wife and grinned. "Guess breakfast is going to be a little late this morning."

"Not for Charlie," Teddy said, setting off another fit of hysteria.

After breakfast, Teddy insisted they take Otis to meet his new friend and sit on the top of the world. "Teddy, it's raining pretty hard," his mother said.

"We have rain slickers and boots," Teddy countered.

Caroline looked at Otis. "Are you going to help me out here?"

Otis gave her a mischievous grin. "What, you're afraid of getting wet?"

"Sugar melts, you know," his wife retorted.

Otis let out his belly laugh that always won her over, and she relented.

A half hour later, four yellow slickers of various sizes were trudging up the trail. Teddy stopped at the spot where he'd met the fawn, but she was nowhere in sight. "Maybe she's made of sugar," he said solemnly. Otis raised his eyebrows at Caroline, and both had to hide their amusement. Caroline assured him that wasn't possible, and probably Charlie's presence kept her away. *I need to watch what I say from now on. He doesn't miss a trick.* They found adult deer tracks, which let her know the fawn's mom was alive and well.

Once they reached the top of the ridge, the rain eased, and a light fog hung over the lake, with the tree line rising tall above. Teddy insisted they sit until it cleared, and having humored him this far, his parents obliged. Soon enough, the fog lifted, and Addisen was laid out below like a beautiful family quilt. Caroline looked over at her husband, whose misty eyes were full of pride. She reached for his hand and gave it a loving squeeze. No words were needed. They both understood this land was exquisite, invaluable, part of the air they needed to breathe. *What a prodigious legacy our son will inherit,* Caroline thought.

Teddy broke the spell (or added to it?) by instructing his father to close his eyes to feel like a bird flying over the clouds. Caroline was pretty sure Otis was already soaring.

Chapter VIII

The following weeks flew by in a flurry of activity. Otis worked tirelessly to prepare Addisen for Memorial Day weekend and the start of the season. Between organizing plant deliveries and helping Dan at the store, Emmy was in perpetual motion. Dan was flat out, finishing the store's addition and helping Otis whenever he needed the backhoe. Dolcie stayed long hours with the boys, sometimes putting them to bed, and nightly prepared dinner for both couples. Even Charlie was wearing down, assisting Otis on long days, and making up for lost time with Teddy at night. The only one not thoroughly exhausted was Caroline. Her years in Manhattan had taught her how to flourish in chaos with little sleep; despite the dark circles under her eyes, she glowed.

Caroline put in long days. She finalized the brochure, revised the payroll to cover travel and mileage, and adjusted the schedule to man all their existing and Morris accounts. With the experienced crew in Boston, Cardinal would have to hire local help to cover the established clients. It meant money would be tight for a while, and she and Emmy would travel to sites more often, but it couldn't be helped. *Growing pains,* she thought. It also meant telling Emmy about the mailing already sent ASAP. Caroline figured she could get Emmy onboard by pointing out her dream nursery was approaching reality. At least, she hoped.

By the middle of May, everything was in place, and Caroline and Emmy sat down to coordinate Morris's plant deliveries with the land prep. With the scheduling set, Emmy propped her feet on the desk and leaned her head back. "I'll be glad when the next few weeks are over and Morris and the store are done. I'm fried. And I miss my Caleb."

"I thought the addition was finished," Caroline said.

"It is, but now we've got to re-lay the counters and stock the shelves."

"I'll lend a hand with that. Things are pretty set here for next week."

"That'll be great, thanks. Too much is happening at once. What do you think about holding off on more expansion until later in the season? That way, we'll have the winter to prepare."

Caroline took a deep breath and filled her partner in on the business plan she'd developed and already set in motion. When Caroline finished, Emmy sat up but remained quiet.

"Earth to Emmy, are you there?"

Finally, Emmy spoke. "I thought we agreed: baby steps?"

"We agreed to a small get-together instead of a party," Caroline countered. "Emmy, if we don't act immediately, the opportunity will be lost."

"How long is the guest list?"

"What?"

"The mailing, Caroline. How big a mailing?"

Caroline's nano-second hesitation said it all. Emmy went still. And very red. "Emmy, we go big to optimize the market's potential. The Morris account gives us a brief opening, and we need to act. It will mean your nursery is within reach sooner rather than later. Trust me on this one."

Emmy stood and looked directly into Caroline's eyes. "As a partner, I have complete faith your decisions will be best for the company. As your friend, I pray you will prioritize what's best for our families."

Caroline felt her face flush and a twinge in her heart. "I always have—what makes you think I would ever waiver from that?"

"Intentionally, you never would. But I know you, and I sense a shift, see a gleam in your eye. Be careful that it doesn't become a fire." She went to leave. "I'm going to see my son before I go to the store."

Emmy paused with her hand on the doorknob and turned back, her face still flushed with anger. "And Caroline? Never make such monumental decisions for Cardinal again without consulting me first. We are partners." She softly closed the door behind her, leaving Caroline to process what had transpired. Emmy had never been angry with her, and it caught her off guard.

Knowing there had to be a good reason, she stepped back and reviewed what had happened. *I've always been the business mind, and she the creative genius. What was different this time?* Caroline knew the answer, of course. *I purposely kept her out of the plan until it was in motion because I knew she wouldn't be on board. But I did it for the good of the company.* Caroline had to admit that wasn't the only reason. *Okay, it was for me, too. I knew I held the winning hand and wanted the endorphin high of being all in.*

Begrudgingly, she acknowledged Emmy was right about the shift in her and could understand her wariness, given how selfishly Caroline had handled things. She realized for her two selves to successfully meld, negative habits and knee-jerk reactions had to be overcome. This was not the cutthroat world of big-city advertising but a partnership with her dearest friend.

There was no room for secrecy, and scheming was unacceptable. Full disclosure and, heaven forbid, compromise, needed to be her automatic reflex now. Emmy was right to be angry at the exclusion, followed by the dismissive attitude towards her input. How could Caroline expect Emmy to trust her self-control when she displayed little to none right out of the box? *Crap. I really botched things up.*

With a self-deprecating sigh, Caroline started to lock up. *I'll stop by the store on my way home to say I'm sorry and set a time to talk.* She owed Emmy an apology and needed to confide the feelings behind her behavior, something she should have shared right away. Talking things through always made things clear and doable for the friends.

Caroline, so engrossed in her introspection, hadn't noticed the cardinal watching her through the window. Satisfied with the outcome, the bird took flight.

Chapter IX

Caroline entered the store, found Dan bent over a box of fixtures, and stifled a snicker at the memory it stirred. The first time she and Dan met, he was in the same position, his yummy buttocks tightly clad in jeans, reminding her of a young Bruce Springsteen. A much different Caroline had set her sights on him, until she met Emmy in a most awkward way.

Thinking Dan invited her over to dinner for a rollicking good time, she was floored when his wife answered the door. Oblivious to Caroline's advances, he hadn't mentioned he was married and only thought Emmy could help reconstruct her mother's garden. That memory made her laugh out loud, causing Dan to turn around. "What's so funny," he asked, standing to kiss her cheek.

"I was just remembering our early days and how I met your wife," Caroline said, and Dan blushed. He had heard the story many times, always embarrassed by his lack of perception and cluelessness. "Is she in the back?"

"No. I could sense something was off, so I told Emmy to stay with Caleb; this could wait. Between here and Cardinal, she's had too much work lately and not enough mommy time."

That's not the only thing off, Caroline thought, but left it for Emmy to tell. She took her jacket off and grabbed a boxcutter.

"You don't have to do that," Dan said. "Go home and grab some mom time yourself. Nothing like hugs and tales of their day to right the world."

"So true, but Otis called to say he was taking Teddy and Charlie to Portland for supplies, so I have some time to kill."

The two friends reminisced while they worked. Caroline had discovered the close friendship their mothers shared through the journal; Dan was told of their bond in high school by Meri, Caroline's mom. After learning his mother hadn't died in an accident when he was two years old but of suicide, Dan was confused, devastated, and angry with his father. Meri spent day and night with him to share all the beauty and memories of the mother he never knew and tell of her fierce love for him. She reasoned his father lied to protect him from the painful truth. Was he wrong to do so? Maybe, but Meri was sure it was well-intended.

"Your mom saved my life," Dan said, not for the first time. *And she's still saving mine,* Caroline silently added.

On a lighter note, they talked about the early years when her brother Will and Dan were camp counselors, and Caroline was a reluctant summer resident. "You were the only kid I knew that preferred concrete over pine needles."

Caroline laughed. "That's where the action was; I didn't want to miss anything."

Caleb came running into Dan's arms and ended the conversation. Emmy was right behind him and looked more relaxed than she had in weeks. Surprised to see Caroline, she hesitated. "I didn't expect to see you here."

"I owe you an apology and want to deliver it immediately."

"Yes, you do, and it is accepted," Emmy said.

"When is a good time to talk?" the friends chorused. Laughing, they decided on the morning, and Emmy shooed Caroline towards the door.

"Go spend time with your son. It will set your world back on its axis." Emmy looked lovingly at her son 'helping' his daddy. When Caroline explained that Teddy wasn't home, Emmy said she'd passed Otis's truck on the way over. With a quick goodbye, she was out the door so fast she missed the "Bye, love you" from all the Preaces.

Once home, Caroline wrapped Teddy in a hug and didn't let him go for most of the evening. "I'm going to hold you like a teddy bear."

"I am your teddy bear—a real live one."

"That you are, little man. The best bear in all the land," she said with a kiss. Typically a wiggle worm, her active son was content to sit and read or play Candyland on his mother's lap. *He misses me as much as I miss him,* she thought. *Just a while longer, little one, and our life's pace will slow,* she silently promised. Allowed to stay up past his bedtime, Teddy's eyes were half-mast when Caroline finally carried him to bed. He held onto her neck when she tucked him in and leaned down to kiss him goodnight. She lay next to him, soaking in his innocence. Love radiated from him, permeating through her skin and bringing warmth to every cell in her body. She felt muscles relax for the first time in weeks, allowing serenity to replace her weariness. With her son's breath on her neck and his hand on her face, Caroline drifted into the deep sleep of contentment.

She woke to Charlie's kisses and Teddy's loud whisper asking if she was awake. Cracking one eye open, she saw her husband standing in the doorway, grinning. "Looks like there was a pajama party in here last night."

"Yep, Mommy slept with me and Charlie, and it was so much fun!"

"Well, I bet after all that excitement, you guys could use those chocolate chip pancakes waiting downstairs."

With whoops and woofs loud enough to be heard around the lake, Teddy and Charlie raced down to the kitchen. When Otis bent down to kiss her good morning, Caroline asked why he hadn't roused her last night. "Because you needed the connection." That she did. *He knows me so well, this beautiful man.*

Dolcie arrived, Caleb and Emmy close behind. Otis had cleared his day to help Dan move counters at the store and headed out early. Emmy and Caroline lingered over a second cup of coffee on the deck to hash out what was happening between them. Caroline confided her recent feelings of needing something, not different, but in addition to. She shared her hypothesis of having two selves, and while one side was happy and satisfied, the other was restless. Both needed to be nurtured for her to be genuinely fulfilled.

Caroline reminded her friend of how much she had grown. Her love of family and Addisen, how she valued the treasures of nature, spirituality, and friendship. "I cherish all these things, Emmy, and need them to sustain me. But I can't help how I'm made; I also need a professional objective, something to aspire to. I ask you to trust me, have confidence in my ability to set limits, to remember what's most important. I screwed up this time, Em, and probably will again, but I know I can do this. Just have patience with me, okay?"

Emmy heard the passion in her partner's voice and reluctantly agreed to give it a try. Caroline went to embrace her, and Emmy held up her hand. "Not so fast. I have non-negotiable stipulations and restrictions." She laid them out in a quiet but firm voice. They'd implement a morning meeting to consult and update, ensuring Caroline could never make another significant decision regarding Cardinal without Emmy's input. "And if you ever scheme to ensure an outcome you want or withhold information from me again, we are through."

Caroline was ready to defend herself until she realized that was precisely what she had done. Chastised, she apologized again and said, "Deal." The partners shook on it, then the two friends hugged. Happy to have their first skirmish behind them, they headed for the office.

Chapter X

With the Morris account settled, the two women turned their attention to hiring local help. Once at the office, Caroline phoned the foreman for an update, and Emmy called the nursery to tell them when the next delivery was needed. Going over the numbers, Emmy concurred a local foreman was an unneeded expense but didn't relish the added time away from Caleb to check sites. Caroline felt the same way and tried to ease their minds by stating it was only for a short time and not every day. Emmy was still wistful. "I know, but we've already spent time away preparing for the season, and this will extend it. They need their mommies."

Caroline recalled the night before with Teddy. "And we need them," she said. The pair sat for a moment, then Caroline snapped her fingers. "I have an idea—we can take them to the sites. It's not like we'll be there all day, and they'll love seeing the tractors and such. It can't hurt to try. We can 'hire' them, assign small tasks, and pay them."

Emmy warmed to the idea. "They'll pack a lunch and go to work just like daddy. And learn money management—half to spend, half in the bank. I like it." Caroline thought four was a bit young for finance but left it alone.

With that issue resolved, they mulled over different ways to advertise for help. Cardinal needed a couple of mature experienced landscapers, but for the most part, high school and college students would suffice. They decided to place an ad in the local community college paper, online in the *Portland Press Herald*, and also put up flyers at the nearby high school and vocational school. Emmy suggested the bulletin boards at the store, laundromat, and gas station. *Such a far cry from headhunters and Linkedin,* Caroline mused. Emmy designed the flyer while Caroline put together the ads. It was Saturday in rural Maine, so nothing more could be done until Monday. By mid-morning, they were free to lend a hand at the store.

The ladies were amazed at what the guys had accomplished so quickly. The counters along the back were moved, and new coolers lined the wall. Produce bins ran along the left side, ready to install the misting apparatus. Addisen's first deli counter, albeit small, sat proudly next to the cash register. The rest of the square footage was a hodgepodge of stacked boxes and homeless counters. Dan explained they got caught up rewiring the electricity and routing the plumbing and hadn't set the counters.

Not wanting to waste a free day so close to opening, the women moved boxes out of the way and studied the blueprint. The pair deduced they could readily transfer the counters by prying the molding off both ends and sliding pallet jacks underneath. Every counter was in place by five o'clock, reassembled, and wiped down. Otis and Dan surveyed the completed project, shaking their heads at their wives' perseverance.

Dan and Otis stayed to finish up, and Caroline and Emmy went to relieve Dolcie. As usual, she'd prepared dinner, which allowed the two women to sit and enjoy their sons at play. Emmy asked when Caroline's brother Will and husband Hector were coming for the holiday weekend, and Caroline realized she didn't know. The last few weeks were so hectic they hadn't spoken. *I'll call tomorrow.*

At the sound of Otis's truck, Charlie's ears perked up, accompanied by a nonstop butt wiggle. The guys were home and greeted like heroes returning from war, minus the marching band. They basked in the attention and soaked up the love, even though exhausted.

After a dinner of Dolcie's famous shepherd's pie, Otis and Dan poured a glass of cabernet to unwind, and Caroline and Emmy steeped a pot of herbal tea. Both women had experienced issues with alcohol in the past, and were acutely aware that even one drink could open Pandora's box. Neither one wished to tempt it and no longer felt the need. Otis lit a fire, and the two families comfortably sprawled out in the living room, relaxed, and enjoying the warmth of fire and friendship. While the adults shared stories and laughter, the boys rested their heads on Charlie, trying and failing to keep their eyes open. By ten o'clock, yawns replaced conversation, and all gave in to weariness. "Sleep. If only I could sleep for a week," Dan said. Emmy patted his back and promised him soon.

"We're so close to the end," Otis said. "One more marathon day should finish the job."

"Caroline and I can stock shelves with the boys," Emmy added, and Dan gave her a skeptical look. "Dolcie needs a day off, and we've devised a plan. Trust us." Dan nodded in agreement, too tired to worry about tomorrow. He lifted his sleeping son and took his family home.

Sunday, Teddy and Caleb had the best day ever. They spent the morning stocking and re-stocking the same bottom shelf, got to pick out their favorite candy bar for morning snack, and had a picnic lunch on a blanket-covered flatbed. They took a long nap on sleeping bags in the pop-up tent Emmy erected in the stockroom and got another candy bar for the late afternoon break. When the boys started to get restless, Caroline cut windows in a large box and made a clubhouse where only they and Charlie were allowed.

By the end of Sunday, the coolers, deli, and produce bins were up and running, and the shelves were stocked. All that remained were the perishable items to be delivered by the middle of the week. Dan couldn't believe it. "I never dreamed it would be ready on time, never mind early. I can't thank you guys enough."

"Hey, I could never have cleared and repaired the roads without your help," Otis said. "It's how we operate around here, you know that." With fondness and appreciation, the friends clasped hands and did that half-hug thing guys do. *Indeed it is.*

Chapter XI

onday. *The last week before Memorial Day, and all of Addisen is ready.* Caroline began a luxurious, cat-like stretch, delighted by the thought.

Amazing. Just amazing. She never tired of the pride and unity the community shared every year as they prepared for the season. Everyone worked tirelessly and lent a hand wherever needed. Not just the Addisen/Preace family but the various managers and retirees. Dolcie's extra hours with the boys and making dinners. Her husband Bert and his fishing buddies helping to clear the campgrounds and get the rental equipment out of storage. Their wives lending a hand with cleaning the bunk houses and rental cabins. Without the summer help (which arrived in June), it would be impossible to accomplish without the group effort. It was as if the whole town melded into one entity, with multiple helping hands and a single-minded goal: Addisen. For Caroline, coming from the dog-eat-dog world of corporate America, it was an anomaly at first and an inspiration always.

Best of all, lying next to her was the heartbeat of this magical being, Otis. His sense of fairness and inclusiveness was the entity's motivation, respect, and gratitude, the lifeblood of the townspeople's wholeness. Caroline propped herself on an elbow and traced Otis's stubbled jawline while he slept. She was still overwhelmed at the emotion this man stirred in her at times such as this. The way his very presence steadied her equilibrium and stabilized her mind. *Don't do anything to fuck it up,* cautioned a small voice in her head. *I won't,* promised Caroline, gently kissing her husband's lips. Otis stirred, pulled her to him, and softly, gently, they welcomed the new day together.

★   ★   ★

By the time Caroline and Teddy returned from their morning walk, Emmy had dropped off Caleb and was headed out to post flyers. Already behind, Otis passed her the baton and raced out the door. A panicked Dolcie called to say she was running late, and after assuring her it was fine, Caroline settled the boys and called her brother. "Hey, remember me?" she quipped.

"Vaguely. Aren't you the red-headed spitfire that sets the world ablaze?"

Caroline laughed. "That would be me, brother of mine. Only the world I set on fire is very different from yesteryear. I'm a wife and mom who lives in the woods, makes wreaths, wears dog hair, and smells like Eau de PB&J."

Will paused. "Sis, what's going on with you?"

Will always saw through her like a piece of cellophane; there was no sense in trying to dodge the question. Caroline shared it all with him. Her love of Addisen life, the opportunity the Boston market held, and the adrenaline rush she'd experienced and relished after so long. How she felt strong and confident in her ability to control her drive because of her love and devotion to Otis, Teddy, and Addisen. "I would never do anything to jeopardize our life together," she said.

"But how can I truly be content if I continue to deprive such an essential part of me?"

"You're going to be the death of me, Sis." Caroline tried to cut him off. "Let me finish. But you make a good point. You've never had the incentive or need to know when to reel it in. Your family provides both. Just don't ignore the warning signs when they pop up."

Will could almost hear her roll her eyes. "Like you'd ever let me."

"Just be careful," he warned.

Eager to change the subject, Caroline asked when he and Hector were coming for the big weekend. "I'll be there on Thursday to beat the traffic and help with last-minute preparations. I'm not sure of Hector's plans."

This time Caroline's sibling antenna went up. Will and Hector always knew each other's agenda.

A renowned custom cabinet and furniture maker, Will was flannel shirts and earthy, and Hector, a savvy New Yorker, was all about fashion and flash, much like their personalities. They lived on a farm Will had restored in Risedale, Connecticut. The town's mixture of artists, horse breeders, and suburbanites gave it an eclectic atmosphere, making it a good fit for Will. As for Hector, Risedale's biggest draws were Will and its location—less than sixty miles from Manhattan. Unlike Will, Hector, born and raised in NYC, sometimes craved the fast-paced, cultural melting pot he grew up in. The city's rudeness, grime, and overpopulation Will groused about was part of the Big Apple's charm to Hector. The couple was proof positive opposites attract, and the combination left many people shaking their heads. But they clicked the moment they'd met in Caroline's office a decade ago and have defied the odds ever since. Caroline had never known the relationship to be any less than solid.

"What do you mean you don't know?" she asked.

Uncomfortable, Will cleared his throat. "He's been in the city since the end of April, and we haven't spoken much."

"Will, what the hell?"

"We'll talk this weekend. I don't want to get into it over the phone. Now let me get back to work. Love you and see you Thursday." Before Caroline could react, he'd hung up. *This is not good.*

Four years ago, when Hector followed Caroline out the door at PG&G, Otis appointed him to oversee the family's city-based charities, which allowed Hector to continue his occasional NYC fix. Her brother-in-law would stay in her old apartment for a few days at a time, but never for a week, much less a month. *Not good at all,* she concluded.

Caroline's thoughts were interrupted when a harried Dolcie flew through the door. "I'm so sorry. I got distracted by something this morning, and time got away from me, and—"

Caroline stopped her as she helped her out of her coat. "No worries, Dolcie, it happens. It gave me a chance to call Will and catch up," *such as it was,* she added to herself. Still distracted, Dolcie gave Caroline's hand a pat and a "That's nice, dear," and went in search of the boys. *What the hell is going on? Will and Hector are on the outs, and Dolcie is frazzled and preoccupied.* Something was chipping away at all she viewed as rock solid. In a hurry to get to work, Caroline threw her jacket on as she went out the door and, so engrossed in her thoughts, failed to see the cardinal pacing on the deck railing like a worried mother.

Chapter XII

Emmy returned to the office to find her partner lost in thought. Caroline relayed the morning's events when Emmy asked if everything was okay. Ever the optimist, Emmy pointed out all marriages go through rough spells, and Will and Hector would work it out if there was an issue. Unlike Caroline, she wasn't convinced there was. On the Dolcie front, however, she shared her friend's concern. Emmy recounted an incident at the store that Dan found odd. Dolcie, picking up an order, got a phone call. Visibly upset, she said she was on her way and rushed out without the groceries. An hour later, worried and unable to reach her, Dan closed the store and delivered the order. Bert answered the door smiling, not a care in the world. Dolcie came out of the kitchen and apologized for her abrupt exit but offered no explanation. Dan said it looked like she'd been crying, but everything appeared okay, and respecting the private person she is, Dan didn't pry. Emmy and Caroline decided it was probably the frenetic pace and long hours of the past weeks wearing her down. After all, they were half her age, and it affected them. "She's such a force of strength and energy, we forget she's in her seventies," Caroline said.

"True," Emmy agreed, "but let's keep a close eye on her.

She wouldn't complain or share her troubles, even if she needed help."

Caroline suggested a solution. She'd spend mornings at the office and Emmy at the store. At 3:00, they would alternate, relieving Dolcie and working at the store. That way, Cardinal stayed on schedule, Dan could keep the store open while receiving deliveries, and Dolcie's day would be cut in half. The biggest problem? Getting Dolcie to agree. Emmy pointed out her pride and stubbornness and feared she'd see it as an insult. While Emmy foreshadowed a Dolcie fit, Caroline pooh-poohed it. "No one is more stubborn than me; I can out-tantrum the best," she stated straight-faced. Emmy couldn't argue that, and the friends went to talk to Dolcie. Much to their surprise, she readily agreed. "Going home earlier would be much appreciated, thank you," she said, teary-eyed. The friends exchanged a worried look. Something was off with Dolcie.

★   ★   ★

The days flew by, and before Caroline could blink, her brother Will was in the driveway. As she had since childhood, she ran to meet him and flung herself into his arms to be spun around and receive the kind of bear hug only a brother can give. Will had no time to recover from his sister's love attack before he was bowled over by two soaked lake rats, one with swimmies and the other with fur. "Uncle Will, you're here! You're here! We're gonna play hide and seek, go swimming, play catch, make s'mores, see fireworks…"

Laughing, Caroline stopped the verbal onslaught. "Let Uncle Will get settled before you plan his entire visit."

Otis came up from the lake and heard Teddy ask where Uncle Hector was. Will looked to his sister for help, but his brother-in-law saved him. "Uncle Hector is taking care of

Daddy's work in the city, so I can stay here," Otis said. Will shot him a grateful look and mouthed thank you. "Now let's get you some dry clothes and Uncle Will a cold beer."

While Otis raced Teddy back to the house, Caroline looped her arm through Will's, and they strolled behind. "Don't think I'm letting you off that easily," she said.

Will gave her a wry look. "Let Uncle Will get settled before you..."

"Fair enough, but tomorrow we talk," she pouted.

"Deal." He kissed the top of her head and, with a gleam in his eye, added, "Race ya," and took off running. "No fair," Caroline yelled and ran to catch him.

After dinner, Will tucked Teddy and Charlie in while Caroline and Otis cleaned up. Preoccupied with her brother's marriage, Caroline was unusually quiet. *I need to know what's going on so I can fix it. Will's always there for me, and now I can help him.* As if reading her mind, Otis gently broke into her thoughts. "When you talk to him, please tread softly. Remember, he's not made like you; he comes from a different place within. What works for you won't for him. He contemplates, you tackle." Caroline wanted to object but couldn't argue with the truth; she and Will had temperaments that were unalike. She promised to keep that in mind as her brother came downstairs.

Seeing the worry on Caroline's face, Will relented. "Okay, we'll talk tonight. No sense in you losing sleep over this." Otis offered to give them privacy, but Will shook him off. "You're family, Otis, like a brother to me. Please stay." Will took a deep breath and did his best to explain the situation.

Until recently, Hector seemed content with their life in Risedale and spending a few days here and there in the city. But now, pushing middle age, he and his city friends no longer hit the clubs and partied until the wee hours. Their get-togethers were quiet brunches, Broadway shows, or intimate dinner parties at someone's loft. Hector increasingly pressured Will to join him for the city stays. He pointed out the difference in activities, and the calmer pace was more conducive to Will's style. Will countered that the city was still the city. NYC unnerved him and altered his well-being. Hector had known from the beginning that Will hated it. Discussions turned into heated debates and, finally, arguments. Hector felt Will was being unfair, refusing to compromise when he, Hector, had sacrificed to move to Risedale years ago. Hurt by the word sacrifice, Will accused Hector of reneging on their agreement. Cut by the word agreement, Hector called Will cold and self-centered, and Will lashed back with a whiny bitch. Things deteriorated from there, and they decided a break was needed.

"But how can you work things out if you aren't talking?" Caroline asked.

"Words escalated the issue, Sis. Sometimes silence is best for a while."

Caroline was frustrated. "You've got to communicate to resolve anything. You can't let this fester."

Otis cleared his throat to interrupt her. Remembering their conversation, she stopped herself and crossed the room to her brother. "I'm here for you, I love you, and I will do my best to bite my tongue." That last bit received a guffaw from both men, and they placed a five-dollar bet on how long it would last. Playing along, Caroline stuck her tongue out and asked if it was bleeding.

"No, but it will be," Otis said.

Laughing, Will rose to go to bed. "Right now, I need a good night's sleep and a few days of hard outdoor labor." Otis assured him there was plenty of that to go around. The work-day started at 7:00am, with breakfast at 6:00. With a salute, Will said his goodnights and went to bed.

Chapter XIII

Caroline and Otis turned in shortly after Will. The couple lay in bed, too tired to make love but too wound up to sleep. Otis tried to set his wife's mind at ease, and Caroline appreciated his attempts to calm her angst, but it wasn't having an effect. Restless, she decided to trade the bed for her mom's old rocker in search of the solace it inevitably provided. Once tucked into the cozy warmth, Caroline reached for her journal and began to untangle her knot of thoughts and fears.

This upset between Will and Hector is so disquieting for me, far beyond sisterly concern. Why? Time to organize my mind's junk drawer and find the missing key.

I know their love is genuine. I can't imagine it won't survive its first challenge. But I've never seen Will so stubborn and unyielding. That was always my forte, and I'm uncomfortable with this sibling role reversal. Can I be a constructive yet loving guide for him, as he's been for me since childhood? That thought makes me smile. Me, setting Will's head on straight. Craziness. I'm determined to do it, though. I will succeed by following the emotional manual he's always used on me: listen, support, but don't hold back, good, bad, or otherwise. Deliver what is needed but emphasize it comes from a place of love. Note to self: remember to stay calm and steady in the delivery.

They have never fought before, not even a squabble. Will and Hector's love and mutual respect for one another's preferences have always trumped any inconvenience their differences caused. Or has it? Has Hector, knowingly or unknowingly, harbored resentment towards Will all these years for the move to Risedale? It was a sizeable accommodation, considering how he loves city life. Will always understood his husband's need for time in the fast lane and supported Hector's time away, but that seems small compared to Hector's epic compromise. Hector's request of Will is much less a concession than he made over a decade ago. Surely my brother will see that when he cools off. Or will he? Because things have gone his way from the beginning, will he see no need for change? Things worked out beautifully for him all these years, and he assumed Hector was also content. After all, Hector never gave any inkling he was no longer satisfied with the status quo.

And therein lies my problem, the reason I'm so distraught. I see the potential for Otis and me to play out a similar scenario. I've caged my enterprising drive since the onset of our relationship. Will Otis understand my need to give it freedom and believe it is tamed enough not to run wild? Will he trust me? Believe in me? Understand it's part of me?

There is only one way to find out: talk to him. I need to level with Otis about my recent feelings and convince him I'm capable of control. My ambition is no longer a beast but a support animal I need to complete myself. I will learn from Hector's silence and have the conversation with my husband sooner rather than later. After this weekend's festivities.

Calm now that she'd found the missing key and satisfied it had opened the correct psychological box, Caroline was ready for bed. Tomorrow was the last day to prep for the celebration of Memorial Day. The weekend promised a whirlwind of activities, and she and Otis were at the center. Not only did they participate in and enjoy the revelry, but the couple also ensured everything went as planned. Caroline loved it.

It was as if Addisen, a grand dame, woke from winter hibernation to don her elegant finery made of exquisite shades of green, accessorized with baubles of budding wildflowers and sun-sparkled diamonds on the lake. A splash of her signature perfume of pine and earth with hints of sweet berries, and she was in splendid form. Memorial Day weekend was when she opened her arms to welcome all of life, furred, feathered, and two-legged, into her bosom for an embrace like no other.

It took Caroline years to discover and appreciate the gift, but she was grateful for her mother's journal and spirit, which opened her heart to the essence and wonder of the natural world. Marrying Otis had only intensified her feeling of love and reverence for Addisen. It was now a part of her, and her son's blood.

Her thoughts sorted, Caroline decided to end the day with the creative vision of Dame Addisen. Stifling a yawn, she switched off the reading lamp and headed to bed.

★ ★ ★

Friday, the sounds of shouted greetings, laughter, and children's squeals of play mingled in harmony and echoed across the lake. With three perfect Maine days forecasted for the weekend, campsites sold out, rental cabins were booked, and families traveled to open their summer homes. Word spread quickly about the renovated general store, and by late afternoon, Dan was scrambling to keep shelves stocked, grateful he had increased orders when he'd heard the weather. By evening most were settled in, and a palpable quietude blanketed the lake like a fog after an active storm.

After dinner, Otis jogged out of the house, eager to make a final round, happy to be back in full swing. Not surprisingly, Teddy chose his uncle to read his bedtime story, so Caroline took her tea to the deck. She watched as campfires were lit around the lake, reminding her of footlights on a stage. Above, the heavens held thousands of twinkling stars, growing brighter as the sky deepened to black. *Angel lights to guide our way,* Caroline thought. The moon, not quite full, reflected on the lake, a spotlight to showcase the beauty of it all. *Dame Addisen, a showstopper. Always giving her best for all to savor, deserving of the love she inspires from here and above.* "Care to share those thoughts you're lost in?" Will asked, sitting beside her. When she did, he gave his head a slight shake and smiled. "Who'd have thought my kid sister would become awakened and a nature lover."

Caroline nodded in agreement. "I know. It's really affected me, how deeply I feel, my ability to trust others, and a sense of belonging to something bigger than myself. It's strange how it has humbled yet strengthened me." When Will teased that she'd always been strong-willed, Caroline corrected her older brother. "I mean, inner strength. The ability to process and evaluate before acting. Self-control is a by-product of self-awareness, I believe."

Will squeezed her hand. "Well, it's an exquisite addition to your personality trousseau. I like this softer side."

Decidedly switching to a different topic, Caroline asked if he'd spoken to Hector and added she hoped to see him this weekend. She felt her brother tense as he responded. "He's spending the weekend in Southampton with Joel and Cameron at their new summer home."

Caroline chose her words carefully. "That sounds nice. And it would be an opportunity to get to know his friends outside the city you abhor."

"We come here on Memorial Day. He knows how much it means to me. It used to mean something to him."

"Nothing wrong with changing it up a little, and bonding with his friends must mean a lot to him," Caroline tried.

"I don't like ultimatums."

"Sounds more like a request to me. Maybe you should compromise on this issue for your marriage's well-being."

Will abruptly stood. "I'm going upstairs to read," he snapped and exited without a goodnight.

Well, that didn't go as planned. I need to work on my approach. Apparently, I'm not the only one uncomfortable with the role reversal. Downhearted, she went in to warm up her tea.

Chapter XIV

The weekend was a monumental success, a page from America's past. Saturday's barbeque provided hot dogs, hamburgers, potato and macaroni salads, baked beans, and watermelon. There were games of badminton, volleyball, corn-in-the-hole, and horseshoes. Saturday night hosted a beach bonfire with sing-a-longs and s'mores. Sunday offered organized races: relay, 3-legged sack, egg on a spoon, canoe, swim, and kayak. It was all capped off with a spectacular fireworks display over the lake, whose water captured the bursts and reflected them back towards the sky, suspending Addisen in a kaleidoscope of light and color. Teddy made sure everyone knew the next fireworks, on his birthday, were just as awesome. Born on the Fourth of July, he was young enough to believe all the fanfare was for him, something the adults happily indulged.

Monday was clean up, and by Monday evening, everyone was in a state of contented exhaustion, none more so than the Addisens. Even Teddy and Charlie were worn out from the nonstop festivities. Will was too tired to drive and wanted to avoid traffic, so he chose to leave in the morning. When he didn't reappear after tucking Teddy in, Caroline went up to find him sleeping with his arm draped protectively over her son. *Always taking care of us.* She tiptoed over to the bed, covered her brother with a blanket, kissed Teddy's cheek, and gave Charlie a pat on the head. "Thanks for watching over them, boy," she whispered. Charlie briefly opened one eye in acknowledgment and was asleep before she closed the door.

Caroline found Otis on the deck, hands behind his head, perfectly still. She knew this was one way he bonded with his land, listening closely as it spoke its unique language. She quietly sat on the chaise beside him and joined in his meditation. With the weekenders and summer residents headed home to wait out the school year, Addisen was serene once more. The breeze blowing through the trees and over the lake reminded Caroline of a fatigued mother letting out a tired but happy sigh.

"Thank you," Otis whispered.

"For what?"

"For loving this place as much as I do. For loving me."

"You're welcome," she said through a half smile.

Otis let out a laugh. "That's milady—always keeping me on my toes."

"Someone has to keep you from getting a big head," she softened with a kiss on his cheek. Caroline scooched Otis over and joined him in his chair. "To the moon and back, and you know it."

Otis kissed the top of her head. "Uh-huh."

This is an excellent time to tell him my revelation and insight into my missing piece. He just acknowledged my love for him and Addisen; undoubtedly, he'll believe I won't do anything to jeopardize that. Caroline took a deep breath to begin the conversation, but Otis started to relive the weekend's highlights, enjoying the good feelings for a second time.

He also shared an incident that had unsettled him. Bert was preparing for the canoe race and asked Teddy if he wanted to join him. Dolcie lost it, pulled Teddy to her, and blurted, "No way." Bert looked humiliated and reminded her their boys canoed with him at Teddy's age. "That was then, and this is now," she said. When she turned to walk away, Otis saw the panic in her eyes. "Something is definitely going on," he said. Caroline reiterated her concerns, and they held each other a little closer.

Otis switched to their favorite subject, their son. "I love that Teddy thinks the Fourth of July hoorah is just for him. It'll be sad when he loses that innocence. We'll have to ensure he knows sharing a birthday with America is a special honor."

Caroline kissed him tenderly. "You were born to be a father, you're a natural." *Now's a good time.* In the split second that thought took, Otis spoke.

"Speaking of which, I've been thinking… Teddy turns five this year. Think it's time for a brother or sister in the making?"

He wants a baby, now? A baby? Sure, another child would be lovely once I get my footing and we navigate the new path together. But not right away. Crap, talk about lousy timing… I need to regroup before I broach the subject with him now.

Otis had felt her body tense. "Don't you want more kids?"

"Of course, but what's the hurry?" Otis reminded her how close she and Will were and what they added to one another's life. Didn't she want that for Teddy?

"Besides, look how much fun it'll be trying." He untangled himself, stood, took her hand, and led her to bed. "No time like the present," he said.

Fuck.

After their lovemaking, when Otis fell asleep, Caroline grabbed her journal and took it to the deck. She needed the chill of the night air to think clearly and sort things out.

That was a shock, though I should have seen it coming. Otis has a point; we don't want too big an age

gap between our children. But one more year isn't so bad, is it? That will give me time to acclimate my world to accommodate everyone's needs, theirs and mine. Am I being selfish? No, I don't believe so. How can I give them my best self if I'm incomplete? And my family deserves all I am. I want to provide them with that and more, something Otis should comprehend. I need to present this in a way he'll understand and believe in me. Present this to my husband.

Like I'm trying to sell a client a concept. I guess that's what it comes down to; trying to get him on board with an idea he isn't going to readily embrace. Am I not giving him enough credit? Maybe not. It's something to think about....

My husband just announced it was time to have a baby, countered my misgivings with a touch of guilt, and promptly led me upstairs to work towards his goal. I'm irked. Am I wrong to be put off by it? No, but per-haps a little harsh. Part of what annoys me is I will-ingly went along with it. Why? Because I was caught off guard or preparing for a much different conversation? Some of each, I suppose. Regardless, his baby wish has complicated the discussion and upped the urgency to talk. Tomorrow is the day.

Caroline closed the journal and noticed the cardinal pacing the railing. "I know you're worried, Mom. But Will and I grew up witnesses to your solid marriage and we saw how it's done. We will make ours work by the example you and Dad set."

Unconvinced, the bird continued to fret.

Chapter XV

After a quick breakfast and lengthy goodbyes, Will was ready to drive back to Connecticut. Caroline walked him to his truck, reluctant to let him go. "I'm worried about you," she said. Will assured her he was fine. "You are not fine. You're living apart from Hector and not communicating, a lethal combo for relationships. Will, you need to reach out to him and fix this."

Will looked down at her. "And you need to leave my business to me."

"How can I when you're so royally screwing up?" *Forget holding my tongue. This is too important.*

Will's look turned into a scowl. "Say you. Chances are, I better know what's best for me."

His tone cut Caroline more than his words, and she matched his anger. "Really? Losing all that's right between you two, the life you've built, the years of love, memories, and family, that's better for you than a lousy compromise on something so important to him?"

"It's more than a lousy compromise. It's a lifestyle change."

"Occasionally. Nothing like the move to Risedale was for Hector. Will, even in your anger, you must see that undeniable fact. You need to be open-minded and fair to be equal partners. You know that. It's not like you to be unreasonable and stubborn."

Will slammed the truck door and revved the engine. "You talking to me about unreasonable and stubborn? Priceless." And with that, her brother left her standing in the empty driveway. *So much for me staying calm and collected to deliver sound advice. This is really eating at him; his buttons are never that easily pushed.*

Caroline turned and walked towards the house to call Hector. *Screw it; this is no time to start minding my own business.* Hector's phone went to voicemail. She left a message to call her ASAP and signed off with "Love you" to let him know she did.

Once at work, she checked with the foreman on the Morris project, was told it was ahead of schedule, and decided to start the follow-up calls that afternoon. Emmy returned from assessing the local jobs and found no major problems. "It's basic clean-up," she reported, which made the temp hiring much easier. College classes had ended, so they contacted the best applicants and scheduled interviews within the next couple of days. The partners hoped to have a crew working by the following week. *Things are moving quickly; I really need to talk to Otis soon.*

At 2:30, Caroline stuffed the mailing list into her briefcase and went to relieve Dolcie. She found her, a sleeping boy tucked under each arm, eyes closed. When Caroline patted her arm and softly called her name, Dolcie jumped as if she'd shouted in her ear. "I'm sorry. I didn't mean to startle you," Caroline said.

"No harm done. I must've dozed off. I haven't been sleeping well."

Caroline sat down next to her. "Dolcie, are you ill? You aren't yourself lately, and we're concerned."

"I'm healthy as ever. You needn't worry about me; I'm a tough old broad."

"Well, something's going on with you, so let's have it."

Dolcie affectionately patted her leg, accompanied by a stern look. "I appreciate the concern, but my business is mine alone. Now let me get home to my husband." Seeing her discomfort, Caroline let it go for now. *Being told to mind my own business is wearing thin today.*

While the boys finished their nap, she intended to start the follow-up calls, but Hector phoned.

"Hector, what the hell is going on with you two?" was her greeting.

He gave a sad huff. "More than should be, considering. I assume Will talked to you over the weekend?" She told him yes but felt there had to be more to it. Once Caroline filled him in on Will's story, Hector's reply surprised her. "That about sums it up."

"Seriously? I don't see where you're asking that much. And it's so unlike him to be unreasonable."

"There is more to the issue, sister-in-law, but I believe it has to do with Will's security in who and what he is, not our relationship."

Caroline wasn't buying it. "Hector, that's crazy. Will came out his first year of high school and never looked back." Hector was so quiet Caroline thought he'd hung up. "Hello? You still there?"

"Yes. I'm trying to organize my thoughts before I speak; this is complicated." Caroline gave him time to find his words, and finally, he spoke. "Will came out but never fully embraced a gay lifestyle."

"He's married to you, for Christ's sake."

"Yes, but our life in Risedale mirrors any straight couple's outside of our sexual orientation. It's a very 'normal' existence that Will feels comfortable in."

Caroline disagreed. "He's always been comfortable in his gayness."

"Really? Did your brother go to his prom? Ever bring a college date home for the holidays? How many relationships did he share with the family? No, Caroline, he's comfortable with the knowledge of being gay but not in his gayness; there is a difference. My NYC friends live very openly, and I believe that scares the bejesus out of him."

"But it's not like you're asking him to lather up in baby oil, put on a pair of hottie shorts, and jump on a float in the gay pride parade."

Hector snorted. "Good God, no! But to Will, maybe what I'm asking feels just as extreme."

"What can I do to help?"

Hector sobered. "Nothing, sweetie. He needs to work through it and come to terms on his own."

"And if he doesn't?"

Silence.

"Hector, this sucks."

Hector's voice cracked. "And then some. Love you, sweetie, take care," and he hung up.

She had always seen Will as quietly confident. Was Hector right, and that perceived confidence wasn't strength but a façade to keep one foot in the closet? Accepting himself for who he was but not fully embracing it? That thought broke her heart. All these years, she'd seen Will as a hero, standing for his true self, devil be damned. Had she been wrong? Hector made a valid point: Will had never brought a date home or spoken of a relationship until Hector, and that was easy for him; Hector worked for Caroline, and she witnessed it happen. She needed to talk to Will but knew enough to let him cool off from the morning's argument. *Arguing with Will.* She couldn't remember a previous time that had happened.

Before Caroline could further contemplate the issue, two preschoolers woke from their nap, ready for a snack and some rambunctious playtime. Much too soon, Emmy was at the door for Caleb, and Otis was home for dinner. "These little guys know how to get every second out of the day," Caroline quipped as she dropped into a chair, feigning exhaustion. Gleefully, the boys tugged on her arms, saying, "More, more," until Otis scooped them up and threw one over each shoulder.

"Where would you like your sack of potatoes delivered, ma'am?"

"The car seat, please," Emmy said. Caroline walked her to the truck, kissed Caleb goodbye, and requested her sack of potatoes be delivered to the sink to wash up for dinner. While they ate, Otis filled her in on his day, and she told him the latest on Dolcie. Relaxing over espresso, Caroline shared the morning argument with Will, and the phone call to Hector, including his theories and her concerns. Otis listened intently, without comment. When Caroline finished, he cautioned her again to tread lightly and respect Will's boundaries. "That's it? No advice or helpful insight?"

"If Will or Hector asks for either, I will gladly give it. For you, milady, my advice is the aforementioned."

After rehashing all the day's traumas, Caroline was emotionally exhausted, too tired to have such a consequential conversation with Otis. *Tomorrow,* she promised herself. Otis spotted the Boston mailing list on the kitchen island while turning out the lights for bed. "What's this?"

"Just work stuff I didn't get to. It's not important." *Seriously, talk to him tomorrow.*

Chapter XVI

Emmy and Caroline, engrossed in the interviews, missed lunch. By 2:00, they had hired half a crew but were famished. As if on cue, Dan came through the door with deli sandwiches, chips, and iced tea. "My hero," Emmy said with a kiss. With a mouthful of chips, Caroline patted her heart and pointed to him in thanks. "How did you know?" his wife asked.

"I didn't but figured you two would get so involved you'd forget to eat. So, how'd it go?"

They updated him between bites of sandwiches, their excitement ringing in every word. "Looks like we'll meet our goal of next week. Two crews. Who would've thought?" Emmy shook her head in disbelief.

"We did," Dan and Caroline said in unison.

Emmy smiled. "So, how's your day going, handsome?"

Dan had left a part-timer at the store to help Otis clear land for the campground expansion. "It was great to have 'man-o-man-o' time with my best buddy," he said. The ladies exchanged a look. "What?"

"Man-o-man-o?"

Dan shrugged and mimed a swoon. "Okay. A joy to share heart-to-heart conversations with a kindred soul I love. Better?"

"No," they chorused, laughing.

After Dan left for the store and Emmy went to relieve Dolcie, Caroline got ready to work on the call list. Reaching down for her briefcase, she didn't see Otis come in.

"Looking for this?" he asked. His body language and quiet tone unsettled Caroline.

"For what? What's going on, Otis?"

Ignoring the question, Otis walked to the door, locked it, flipped the open sign to closed, silenced the ringer on his phone, and gestured for her to do the same. Only then did he place the list on her desk. He tapped it twice with his fingers as if to make it magically disappear and sat down across from her. "You tell me."

This is not how I wanted this to go down. "That's a call list for Boston and the surrounding suburbs."

Otis's eyes bore into hers. "To follow up on the mailing you sent out weeks ago. To expand Cardinal Design. Without telling me, much less discuss how it will affect our family."

"Otis, I've wanted to talk to you for weeks, but it never seemed the right time, what with Will, Dolcie, and Memorial Day..."

Otis interrupted her. "No time like the present." *He's really pissed.* "But before you begin, know that Dan has filled me in on all the exciting things happening with Cardinal, so keep it honest. Evidently, some wives share important matters with their husbands."

"Otis, you're angry right now. Maybe this isn't the best time for us to talk."

He just sat there waiting. And stewing. And waiting some more.

Okay, I guess we do this now. Caroline took a deep breath and dove in headfirst, explaining her a-ha moment and the feelings it stirred. How it led her to realize a vital part of her was neglected but needed to complete her. And tried to assure him she'd never be consumed as before because he, Teddy, and Addisen were now her world; faith and self-knowledge her axis. She promised never to do anything to endanger their well-being or stability and asked that he trust her.

"Trust you? Right out of the gate, you kept your intentions from me, followed by hiding any forward progression of your plan."

Caroline stood, her fists clenched. "I explained what happened. I wanted the time to be right for a calm discussion."

"Was it that, Caroline, or fear I wouldn't be on board, so you forged ahead without me to assure you'd get your way?"

Caroline shook her head. "I wanted to explain it in a way you'd understand. I knew you would have reservations, but I didn't intentionally hide it from you or avoid the conversation. The timing was bad, is all."

Otis was too angry to be convinced. "Not buying it. And what about the baby? I thought we decided it was time to have more kids."

"No, *you* decided it was time. I wanted to wait."

"Now I know why."

"One year, Otis. I'm asking for one year to prove I can do this."

Without another word, Otis left, slamming the door behind him.

Too unnerved to work, Caroline grabbed a notepad and went to sit on the dock to journal.

As with Emmy, I handled this all wrong with Otis. He's right to be upset, not to trust I have a handle on things. I plowed over both of them. I need to check

myself before every move for a while. I guess old ways are hard to overcome. I've come far, but this is my first test professionally, and it will take more than I anticipated to hold the line. But hold it, I can and will. Meanwhile, I gave myself a mountain to climb with both my partners. Emmy was quick to forgive me and give me a shot. But will Otis afford me the same? Looking at it from his angle, I can see why he's upset. I didn't realize so much was set in motion with him still in the dark. Is he right, and I avoided talking to him out of fear? Or to get my own way? Maybe. Okay, yes, in part. I was waiting for the perfect time to better my chances of turning him around. Instead, I made matters infinitely worse by losing his trust. Will I forever be a work in progress? Yes, I believe that is my fate. Fortunately, I love a good challenge.

Caroline returned to the office, tucked the entry into her briefcase, and locked up. She had to talk to her husband, and this time, she wouldn't wait.

Caroline found Emmy, not Otis, at home. Emmy told her he'd called, said something had come up, and asked her to stay.

Caroline sank into a chair and filled Emmy in on what was happening. "So, he learned nothing from me and everything from Dan this morning," she finished.

Flabbergasted that Caroline hadn't told her husband, Emmy agreed she had screwed up royally. She understood the reasoning behind waiting for the right time and Caroline's concern that Otis might not readily agree. But Emmy could also see where Otis was blindsided, angry, and unsure of his wife's transparency.

"He feels betrayed. You've got to make him believe he can still count on you for the truth and convince him you have a handle on things." Emmy wished her friend luck and left before her cousin got home. The Addisens were going to need some privacy.

Chapter XVII

It was after 9:00pm when Caroline heard Otis's truck pull into the drive. He came in, grabbed a bottle of water and leaned against the counter, arms crossed as though to protect himself from what was about to happen.

"I was getting worried," Caroline said.

"I needed time to download, process, and cool off."

"And?"

Otis rubbed his face. "I have questions."

"Okay." *Please, God, let me have the answers.*

"Why, after all this time?"

"I don't know; I suppose various things are coming together at once. Teddy getting older, I'm secure in the fact I can keep things in perspective, and the Morris account provided an unforeseen opportunity. Beforehand, my only option to scratch the itch was to get back in the advertising game, and I didn't want that. I knew our family would pay the price, and it deterred any urges that whispered in my ear. But this is different."

"Feels the same to me."

Caroline disagreed. "I'm adding to our life here, not taking from it. Cardinal's expansion fulfills me without sacrificing my family's or community's needs. Cardinal Design is part of our family and of Addisen. The former risked introducing negative vibes and upheavals to our existence; something I refused to do."

"I thought you were over the self-serving, aggressive, win-at-all-cost shit years ago."

Ouch. Check your temper and stay the course, lady. "I am over the extremism; that's what I've tried to tell you. But my ambitious nature is part of me and not something I can dismiss any longer. Why can't you try to accept it and trust me to do the right thing?"

Otis spread his arms. "Why aren't we enough for you anymore?"

"That's not fair, Otis."

"Nothing about this is fair." Otis pushed away from the counter to leave the room, but Caroline blocked his way. She was about to insist he stay when she heard (remembered?) *baby steps... patience.* Heeding the message, Caroline stepped aside and watched her husband walk away from her for the second time that day.

Caroline's emotions were confused, scared, indignant, sad, torn, and hurt, all balled into a lump that rested in her throat. And her anger at herself and Otis burned in her stomach like a peptic ulcer. Too agitated to go to bed or even journal, Caroline found her way to the library and, in her mom's rocker, rocked to calm herself, much as her mother had done when she was a baby. She thought of nothing for a long time but focused on the back-and-forth sway until she regained her composure. Her equanimity restored, Caroline grabbed her journal to transfer her thoughts from mind to paper.

I know this got off to a bad start, but I explained why and apologized profusely. Yet it's not enough. It's

not like Otis to be contrary or jump to conclusions. Or is it? I remember the summer we met and how we clashed like a pair of cymbals, each assuming the worst of the other's words or actions. But we overcame that, bonded as a couple, and accepted each other for who we were. Or did we? Our life together has followed his dream agenda, with me his ideal wife. Is he afraid this part of me resurfacing will alter that or had he never come to terms with that piece of me and hoped it was gone forever? His cutting comments make me fear the latter. How can he possibly think my family is no longer enough when clearly, they are everything to me? No, he can't believe that; he was striking out. And self-serving, aggressive? He, of all people, knows better than that; I'm different now.

Admittedly, I thought the defensive, biting Otis was gone, and I'm not thrilled to see him back. So, maybe we weren't all accepting as much as blessed with life on a newly paved road. I guess an eventual pothole was inevitable. I'm determined we will steer around it together. I will share these insights with my husband tomorrow and hope he sees some logic in them. As I said to Will, open communication is the key.

With the chaos in her mind cleared and processed into orderly words, Caroline made a cup of tea and sat on the deck. Charlie padded out and curled up on the lounge, his head in her lap. "Thanks for the love, buddy," she cooed, scratching his ears to reciprocate. "You always sense when someone needs cuddles."

Warmed by the tea and her dog, Caroline settled into the

mystical environment surrounding her. The wonder of where they lived never ceased to move her, and she allowed it to engulf her, replacing angst with serenity. She watched the fireflies light the way for their mates and recalled the first time Otis invited her here to dinner. They'd sat on this same deck, the attraction and sexual tension between them igniting sparks that reminded her of fireflies, a memory that warmed her. *It was quite a night.* It marked the beginning and end of so much in her life.

It was the first real test of Caroline's alcohol recovery (which she aced) and the night she and Otis rid themselves of all shields and armor, allowing the sword of passion to penetrate their heart and provide an opening to receive love. It was the start of a mutual bond strong enough to invoke a trust both believed they were no longer capable of. Because of that eventual love and trust, Caroline softened and released the aggression she used to protect herself from vulnerability. She gradually laid herself bare, fully exposed, with no fear of condemnation or abandonment, as did Otis. Recalling all this added clarity for her. *I feel censured, and Otis perceives rejection. We fear the foundation of our relationship, and trust, is compromised. We need to reassure each other it is solid and impenetrable. More insights to share,* she thought.

Snuggled and comfy with Charlie under the blanket of night, Caroline hated the idea of moving but knew it was late. "Well, Charlie, I'd better get some sleep if I'm going to make sense of all this with your master tomorrow." Reluctantly, the pair went inside to bed.

Chapter XVIII

Caroline quietly entered the bedroom so as not to disturb Otis. "I'm awake," he said, startling her. "You're turning in late," he added.

"I needed to sort some things out and make sense of others."

"And?"

"I believe I did. Care to hear?" She chose to take his silence as an invitation to proceed. Caroline related it all: thoughts on their past selves as she journaled and her memories on the deck that led her to ponder the trust issue. Otis remained quiet through it all. When finished, Caroline kissed his shoulder, rolled over, and left him to contemplate her reasoning.

A week passed, and Otis still hadn't responded to Caroline's observations. Her patience was worn thin, but she was determined to wait him out. *He'll have to address it sometime; letting him come to me is best.* Not that there wasn't plenty to occupy her mind. The Boston marketing results indicated promise, the foreman was already scouting potential employees, and the temporary local crew was in place. A cloud of worry over Will, Hector, and Dolcie grayed her thoughts, but Teddy bombarding her with ideas for his birthday provided breakthroughs of sunshine. Still, with the line that tethered her and Otis frayed, her mind wouldn't focus. Caroline's psyche couldn't rest when the core stability of her world, their connection, was in danger of going adrift. *Soon Otis, please,* she pleaded daily.

She staved off resentment by taking long walks at lunchtime, her face to the sun, and filling her lungs with Mother Nature-kissed air, the cardinal never far behind. Towards the end of the second week, Caroline returned from one such therapy session to find Otis on the porch of Cardinal Design. He wrapped her in a hug and whispered, "I miss you. I miss us." Caroline answered with a soft kiss, and they went to sit on the end of the dock.

"I remember the morning Charlie and I found a cup of coffee and peanut butter toast in this spot, a signal you'd come back. When I looked up and saw you sitting on the porch swing, my world was complete, and I thought yours was too." He swept his arms wide. "You'd chosen this, me, over your city life, and that part of you was laid to rest. I understand now that leaving that life behind didn't include that piece of you expiring. I'm not going to lie, Caroline, it threw me; it was—and is—a disappointment." Otis gave a sad smile as he raised his hand to stop her from interrupting. "Not in you, but in my idea of the perfect world of us. That took time to admit." He gave her hand a squeeze. "So much easier to put it all on you."

Otis continued. "The thoughts and insights you shared make sense, especially the trust issue." He rubbed his face and sighed, defeated. "I'm still uncomfortable with it, but recognize it's a need for you. I'll do my best to get on board for one year. Then we revisit the whole thing."

Do his best?

"Otis, we need to approach this as a team for it to work."

He stood to leave. "Trust. I'll trust you won't get carried away, and you trust I won't set you up to fail." He pulled her to her feet and gave her a kiss. "I need to get back to work. I'll see you tonight." *This will be quite the test*, she thought as he motored off. Caroline wasn't feeling as coupled as she'd hoped after their talk. *Talk? More like a monologue.* "Well, it's a start," she said aloud to no one and went in to work.

Between planning for Teddy's birthday, securing appointments with Boston clients, and starting the rotation for local jobs, the weeks flew by for Caroline, and Teddy's big day was around the corner. She was surprised but thrilled when Hector called to say he'd be there for the Fourth of July. "It's Teddy's birthday, what kind of uncle would miss such an event?" Hector quipped. When she called Will to share her excitement, he gave her the vocal version of a shrug. "Yeah, whatever."

"Seems to me he's making an effort." Silence. "Maybe it'll be easier for you two to talk while you're here; it's such a peaceful place." More silence. She swallowed a comment, said her goodbyes, and hung up. *I need to focus on maneuvering through my own relationship obstacle course.*

She and Otis were a functioning couple once again. Still, an air of cautiousness surrounded their interactions as if they were afraid of trampling their newfound mutual ground to mud. Caroline told herself it was temporary, but nevertheless, it was nerve-wracking. She was accustomed to the effortless, natural aura that always surrounded them and hated the recent set of vibes. *I hope we get it back soon. I'll have to travel to Boston for a night or two sometime in July, and it'll be our first challenge; we need to be on solid ground.* Caroline intended to hold off telling Otis until after Teddy's birthday but had to bring it up soon. It was not something she looked forward to.

Thank goodness for Teddy, Caroline thought again. He was

the center square in their small family's quilt and an incentive for both parents to stitch up the tears. His endless chatter and excitement over the upcoming birthday (and life itself) were contagious. Otis and Caroline found it impossible not to connect when engaging with their son. "Daddy, can we have fireworks all day this year?" Teddy asked at dinner.

"Bear, you can't see fireworks during the day," Otis reasoned.

"And what about the parade? You don't want to give that up," Caroline added.

"Oh no, never! Can me and Charlie have a float this year?"

"Where did you hear about floats?"

"Uncle Hector told me there's the greatest parade ever in a big apple, and all the important people get to ride on a float, and there's giant balloons, and bands, and dancers, and Santa Claus comes. Wouldn't that be awesome?"

Thank you, Uncle Hector. "It's in a huge city nicknamed 'The Big Apple,' not in an apple, and millions of people live there. It's a lot bigger than Addisen."

"Oh." All the enthusiasm started to drain from his little body like a balloon leaking air. Unable to stand his disappointment, Caroline and Otis exchanged a quick look and began planning.

"I have an old trailer in the boathouse. I bet Uncle Dan and I could fashion a float out of it. And Mom and Auntie Emmy can decorate it like they do the wreaths."

"Absolutely. And when you and I go to Portland tomorrow to check on a job, we'll stop and buy humongous balloons and helium," Caroline added.

"What's humongous and helium?"

"Humongous is way bigger than giant, and helium is the gas that makes them float."

Teddy pumped his fist in the air. "Yeah, now we're talking."

He asked if they could go to Burger King instead of packing a lunch, so he'd have a crown, and would Auntie Emmy make a sash for Charlie that said, Mayor? Done. Santa was covered by one of the retirees who had the suit, and a donation to the nearby high school band would ensure 'Happy Birthday' was added to their parade rotation. Otis crossed those requests off the list. Caroline promised to provide dancers. *Hector introduced the idea and she'd make sure he came through, even if it meant he had to do the cha-cha behind the float.*

"This is gonna be the best birthday, *evah*!" Teddy said. He jumped around while Charlie barked, and Otis and Caroline's fist bump turned into a passionate kiss. *Thank goodness for Teddy.*

Chapter XIX

Two days before the big event, Caroline and Emmy were putting the final touches on the float, enjoying downtime with each other. They were excited that the business was going as planned on all fronts but hadn't discussed much else in weeks. It was nice to immerse themselves in friendship and catch up on other things.

Emmy shared she felt Dan withdrawing as he did every year around the anniversary of his mother's suicide. She understood her husband's need to reflect on what could have been and grieve the loss but was concerned it had deepened this year. "Why, I wonder?" she asked her friend. Caroline suggested Dan could answer the question better than anyone, making Emmy smile. "You always know the quickest way to get from point A to B. I will ask him tonight."

Caroline talked of the strain between her and Otis and how Teddy eased the tension. Emmy was happy to hear it was less stressful but cautioned not to expect it as the norm for a while. Caroline assured her she wasn't and confided how uneasy she felt about telling Otis of the trip. "Monday night," Emmy advised. Caroline promised she'd learned her lesson and planned on breaking the news after Teddy's birthday weekend.

"Let's hope there aren't indoor fireworks," Caroline said. Emmy put her arm around her friend's shoulders.

"It's a struggle and won't happen overnight, but he'll come around. He loves you."

"Me, or his version of me?"

"You," Emmy said with such conviction that Caroline believed it.

The project finished, they stepped back to appraise their work and doubled over with laughter. Emmy and Caroline had done their best to blend birthday and Fourth of July decorations compatibly, but it was still a gaudy sight. "It might've worked better if his favorite color wasn't orange this year," Emmy giggled.

"It's perfect—Teddy will love it," his mom said.

Checking the time, Caroline realized Hector was due and hustled home. She couldn't wait to hug his neck. The pair had clicked the day Caroline hired him as her assistant at PG&G and grew close as the years passed. Caroline was a bitch in that life, but Hector never feared her or backed down, and she had respected that. Hector was also Caroline's voice of reason when her temper wanted to send her off on a professional tangent, and the only one she trusted at the firm. Caroline shuddered at the memory of the woman she used to be. Angry, aggressive, and ruthless, her sole purpose was to win, and get ahead at all costs. *And let's face it, the only person who could stand me was Hector. How can Otis think I'd revert to that person after spending the last five years with me? He knows the transition I went through and saw firsthand the work I put in to be a better me, to find peace. Did he think it was temporary? Does the man know me at all?*

Her train of thought was broken when she saw her brother-in-law's car in the driveway. Rushing through the door, Caroline found Hector, Dolcie, and the boys on the floor building

Lego rocket ships. "Mommy's home." Teddy came running at full speed. "Mommy, Uncle Hector's here!"

"I can see that," Caroline said as Hector gave her a king-sized hug. "And not a moment too soon. I've missed you."

"Likewise," he said and kissed both cheeks, European style.

Dolcie unfolded herself off the floor like a woman half her age and patted Hector on the arm. "I'll leave you two to it," she said, kissing the boys. "And I'll see you gentlemen the day after tomorrow at nine o'clock for the parade." On the way out, she waved a hand toward Hector's expensive suit and suggested he find a lint brush.

Hector looked down and realized Charlie had left more than love while snuggling against him. "I think the fur adds a designer's touch, don't you, boy?" Charlie danced around in approval. When Caroline asked why Hector hadn't changed into play clothes, he told her his expertise in rocket building was immediately needed, and there was no time for unnecessary delays. Shaking her head, she sent him upstairs to change and helped the boys pick up before Emmy came for Caleb.

Once the excitement of Hector's arrival was under control and the rocket ships secured safely on their launch pads, Teddy had questions. "Why isn't Uncle Will with you?"

"Because he's finishing an important project. He'll come tomorrow." Caroline hoped that was the real reason and things had improved.

"Oh, okay. Where are the parade dancers?"

Caroline couldn't help but smirk. "Yes, Uncle, where are the dancers?" *I can't wait to hear this.*

Hector didn't skip a beat. "They will be here at eight sharp on your birthday, ready to rock n' roll." Hector met Caroline's shocked expression with a smug one. "Have I ever not pulled through?" She admitted he had not. Teddy wanted to know all the scoop: who they were, which song? "That's all a surprise," his uncle said. "You'll have to wait and see. You too, mom." Caroline pulled a pout face that was only half in jest, making Hector laugh. *He knows me so well, my dear, dear friend.* As if he read her mind, Hector gave her a wink, and an air kiss, confirming their connection.

Will pulled in late the following morning, the completed important project in the bed of his truck. It was a small, hand-carved wooden throne painted gold with orange upholstery. Emmy and Caroline agreed it was the perfect finish for the float, adding even more orange to the red, white, and blue theme. Teddy was beside himself with joy, unable to contain his excitement long enough to sit in it more than seconds at a time. He'd plop down, bounce up, hug his uncle, and repeat.

Caroline noticed Will and Hector drift towards one another as they delighted in their nephew's innocent excitement. *Teddy is the epicenter of the love this family shares. He is a reminder of all that's right between us, the accumulation of why we are all together. For him, we must work to close the rifts in our relationships before they become chasms.* Emmy came up beside her. "Penny for your thoughts." Caroline shared them and added an observation: none of her and Otis's or Will and Hector's current issues were insurmountable; none required more than adjustments, a compromise or two. "What seems a small adjustment to one can be monumental for another. Please keep that in mind," Emmy advised her friend.

"You think Hector and I are asking too much?"

"No, but it doesn't matter what I think; it matters what your husbands think."

Caroline looped her arm through Emmy's and sighed. "Good point, thank you," she said, and they joined the others.

Chapter XX

ourth of July. Again. Already. Caroline sat and watched the day dawn on her son's birthday, wondering where the time had gone. On the one hand, she remembered every detail of Teddy's young life. On the other, it felt like he was born just yesterday.

Caroline raised her coffee mug to the sky in appreciation and laid her head back, to fully enjoy the birth of a new day. She never tired of the way the sun's wakening light turned black to gray, and gray to magnificent colors, before bursting onto the sky's stage like the super star it is. A show that never disappoints, is never the same twice. *Just like our Teddy.* She recalled the dawn of her son's first day.

★   ★   ★

Caroline had known she was in the early stages of labor but wanted, needed, to start that day of new beginnings with Mother Nature. Not much rattled her, but the prospect of giving birth and all that could go wrong had her anxious. She'd never felt the intensity of love and protectiveness for anyone as she did for the baby that shared her body. Gently, Caroline laid a hand on her churning belly and spoke quietly to the little one. "I'm just as excited as you are about your arrival but a little apprehensive too. For the first time, you'll be exposed, laid bare to the world, others, and life's elements. I promise to shield you from harm with my every breath." *Please let it be enough,* she had prayed.

The contraction had eased, and Caroline had watched the sky turn into a palette of color as the cardinal landed next to her chair. Peace replaced angst, and composure ousted concern. A grateful Caroline thanked the universe and blew the cardinal a kiss. She looked to the sky, knowing angels were ever-present, surrounding all with love. "We are never alone, baby, never unprotected." After the next contraction, she had hoisted herself from the chair. "Time to wake up Daddy, little one. Apparently, you've chosen today as your birthday, determined not to miss the fireworks."

Teddy was born at 4:44pm, leaving himself time to get checked out, test drive his lungs, have a snack, and nap before the fireworks display. Years later, the vision of Otis holding their son, bathed in bursts of light and color, was as vivid as if it was yesterday. She could still hear him tell Teddy it was all for him, bringing tears to her eyes; his reverent voice had whispered that angels and Addisen were rejoicing together in celebration of his birth.

★   ★   ★

Caroline's nostalgic reverie ended with an ear-splitting whoop and Teddy pounding down the stairs, yelling, "It's my birthday, it's my birthday!" He knew to find his mother on the deck at this hour and raced out to get his first birthday kiss of the day. Caroline wrapped him in a mama bear hug and kissed him till he giggled. "Mommy, stop; save some for later," he squealed.

"I have plenty more where those came from," she assured him. "How does it feel to be five?"

"I'm not really five until 4:44, but we need the whole day to fit in all the fun," Teddy said, parroting his father's words.

So many fours, the angel number. Caroline smiled and silently thanked them for surrounding her son. "True. Let's go down the list." Teddy happily checked each one off on his little fingers. Blowing out the first set of candles on his pancakes after everyone sang "Happy Birthday" at breakfast. The parade. Riding around the lake with Charlie and Daddy in the skiff, holding balloons and blowing the foghorn. The town cookout with games and the gigantic red, white, and blue cake with tons of candles. The bonfire and fireworks. And finally, a cake at home with candles, ice cream, wishes, and presents.

"We better get started!" Teddy rushed in to wake up the rest, while Caroline hoped this wasn't the year he figured out he shared the celebration.

She entered the kitchen to find Otis preparing pancake batter and two sleepy uncles in search of coffee. Hector grumbled something about the crack of dawn, and Teddy pointed to the sun and informed him it had already cracked. Hector laughed and ruffled his nephew's hair; his mood instantly improved. Caroline noticed Will watching the scene with tenderness, *a good sign,* she thought. The Preaces arrived, and the festivities began. Once he'd blown his candles out, Teddy insisted that they relight them so his cousin Caleb could do it too. With bellies full of pancakes, everyone got to work. Will, Dan, and Otis went to organize the parade, Hector disappeared to meet his dancers, and the moms got the boys ready for a full day.

At 10:00 sharp, Addisen's Fourth of July parade started down Main Street to loop around the lake, as it had for generations. Teddy sat on his throne, regal in the Burger King crown, waving to the crowd. And Charlie was splendid in his mayor's banner and a black top hat that Emmy had fashioned from poster board. Not to be left out, Caleb sat beside Charlie, wearing a birthday hat, and blowing a horn. Dolcie stood behind the throne, throwing candy at the spectators to ensure loud cheers as the float passed. Camp counselors walked beside the high school band, sailing five-foot balloons of Elmo, Spiderman, Uncle Sam, and a flag. At the end of Main Street, the parade paused, and the band played "Happy Birthday" as promised.

When the parade didn't march on, everything got quiet. Suddenly, Kool and the Gang's song, "Celebration," blasted through a hidden speaker on the float, and a voice boomed through a bullhorn, "Ladies and gentlemen, we proudly present, straight from New York City, Teddy's Tangerines!" Four dancers in orange face paint came skipping out of the crowd. Two clapped their orange hands over their heads to get the spectators to join in while the others passed out orange streamers on a stick to wave about. The elation on Teddy's face, the shock on Dolcie's, the amusement on Otis's, the total abandonment of the dancers, and the crowd's participation was a cherished moment. Caroline struggled to take it all in at once.

Once things were rockin', the four dancers, dressed all in orange, saved their gigantic hats shaped like a birthday cake, lined up in front of the float, and counted 5, 6, 7, 8... What ensued was a choreographed menagerie of Fosse jazz, Michael Jackson's moonwalk, and some hip hop, all flawlessly performed to the 1980 disco hit "Celebration". *Only Hector could pull this off,* Caroline thought as her heart swelled. She saw her brother watching intently, admiration and love written on his face, and realized Hector was one of the dancers. She barely had time to process the information before the dance ended; they bowed to raucous applause and bowed to Teddy. On cue, Santa appeared, waving a large flag and Ho,

Ho, Ho-ing. He signaled the band to begin, and the parade continued with everyone joining Santa in "You're a Grand Old Flag," the Tangerines marching behind him in unison. It was all perfect, and Caroline couldn't keep her eyes dry. Emmy was also a mess, and the two clapped, cried, danced, and laughed together, happy their sons now had this memory and grateful they had each other.

Chapter XXI

As the parade dispersed and people started towards the cookout, Caroline found Will and Hector talking to the other Tangerines. She introduced herself to Joel, Cameron, and Miguel. "I can't thank you enough," she said, hugging each one.

"Anything for Hector. He's like family," Joel said.

"Plus, we finally meet Will and see this paradise Hector raves about," Miguel added.

"How did you ever come up with the idea?" Caroline was still in awe.

Hector explained how over dinner, they'd talked about different plans for the Fourth, and he stated Addisen's celebration was the best by far. Authentic, heart-warming, communal; a piece of old-time, small town, like it's supposed to be. And Teddy's birthday on the same day made it that much more.

Hector divulged how he'd told Teddy about the Macy's Thanksgiving Parade, in all its splendor, and now his nephew's heart was set on having one of his own.

"I called it a faux pas, but Cameron corrected me," Hector said.

"More like a major fuck-up," Cameron amended, giving his friend an ironic smile and took over the story. "Hector said everything was set except the dancers, and he had no idea where to begin. By then, we had drained the fourth bottle of cabernet and felt quite festive. Joel mentioned he could moonwalk, Miguel bragged he'd won first place in a rec center hip hop competition years ago, and I'd done musical theater in college. We all started doing our thing at once like the drunken fools we were, and before we knew what hit us, Hector declared us his dance team. And that's how Teddy's Tangerines came to fruition—pun intended," he finished with a theatrical bow.

Caroline saw how intently Will watched the friends as they joked around and recalled the fun they'd had rehearsing. They teased one another comfortably, as only best buddies can. *See, brother? There is nothing to fear, just nice guys who genuinely care about one another, enjoy life, and support each other. Friends.* Caroline knew the difference Emmy had made in her life and wanted the same for Will. *We all need a tribe.* The story told, she suggested the group take the skiff across the lake to shower and change into comfortable clothes. Eager to remove the orange body paint, they thanked her and headed toward the lake and a warm shower.

It was hours before Caroline stopped to catch her breath. She noticed Will conversing with Miguel, his body language more at ease, the protective shell chipping away. She watched as Joel taught campers how to moonwalk and saw that Cameron had arranged a cannonball competition off the dock. It was as if they were lifelong summer Addisenites. Hector watched her take it all in, draped his arm across her shoulders, and smiled triumphantly. "Not bad for a day's work, don't you agree?"

"It was genius to invite them here," Caroline said.

"If the mountain won't come to Muhammad, bring Muhammad to the mountain," Hector mused. "Or maybe it's the other way around," he said with a dismissive wave. "Either way, you get the gist."

"It was a gamble. It took a lot of gall," Caroline said with admiration.

"My bubbe, God rest her soul, called it chutzpah, and yes, I have plenty."

Caroline laughed. "That you do, my friend."

"It really wasn't all that daring. The guys are quality people, real. The risk was, would Will give them a chance. I realize there's still a journey ahead, but at least it's a step forward. He can't deny he enjoyed their company today or that they fit into his environment."

After the fireworks, Hector's friends got ready to leave. They'd won the hearts of all of Addisen, and it took an hour of goodbyes before they got in the car. A promise to return, and royal waves, "Celebration" blared through the windows, and the group exited like the superstars they were.

By the time Teddy had his final party and opened his presents, he was half asleep in his cake and ice cream. While Otis carried him to bed, Caroline made tea and headed to the deck, where she saw Will and Hector in deep conversation. With a smile and fingers crossed, she went upstairs to the master suite, where Otis found her sprawled on floor pillows, stargazing through the skylight. He stretched out beside her and put his head in her lap. The couple intimately relived the day, savoring Teddy's reaction to it all. Enveloped in the glow of their son's happiness, they ended the day making love, soft as a whisper and sweet as their boy's innocence. *We are going to be just fine,* Caroline thought as she drifted off to sleep.

★　★　★

Exhausted, everyone slept in the following day, Teddy and Charlie included. Caroline and Will were first up and chose the porch swing for their coffee. They sat in compatible silence and enjoyed the memories and their parents' presence the swing evoked.

"So," Will said after a time. "Hector and I did a lot of talking last night."

"And?"

"We better understand where the other is coming from. Hector believed I was afraid of an openly gay community, and I felt our life together was no longer enough for him. Turns out we were both a little wrong and a bit right."

"How so?" Caroline asked. A kayak passed by and provided Will an analogy to help explain.

"I'm like that kayak; I glide steady and smooth to keep the waters calm and relish all that's along the way. Hector's more of a jet ski, all speed, and motion. Choppy water is no deterrent on his race to the next shore. We approach life two different ways."

"But that's nothing new, and you guys always made it work before. I still don't get some right and some wrong."

"I'm getting there, Sis." Will went on to say he and Hector admitted they jumped to conclusions about the other's motivation. Hector thought Will was ultimately uncomfortable being gay, and Will believed Hector was ready to move on; neither was true. "My aversion to his NYC lifestyle has nothing to do with my sexuality and everything to do with a kayaker hopping onto the back of a jet ski. Hector, who idled while in Risedale, no longer wanted to ride alone when he journeyed on the open water. It had nothing to do with his feelings for me." Will took a breath before continuing.

"We abandoned communication, fed our egos instead, and hurt feelings developed into self-righteousness. We have a ways to go, but at least we're back to open honesty. And Hector is coming home."

With that news, Caroline let out a whoop, and the cardinal chirped from a pine bough above. *At least it's a start.*

Chapter XXII

Early afternoon, Will and Hector left for home, and Otis started his rounds. Still worn out from the day before, Charlie and Teddy were content to laze around the house with Caroline. After a game of Candyland, she put on a Spiderman movie, and the buddies were asleep in no time. She tried to nap, but the need to tell Otis about her trip nagged at her. Things were right between them again, and Caroline feared the distance would return. *Is it worth it? Should I just leave it be?* a tiny voice asked. *Good God, no,* her conscious mind answered. *That little insecure voice needs to be silenced if I'm going to see this through.* And Caroline was determined to do just that. She decided to talk to Otis today rather than wait and eliminate the opportunity for doubt to speak again. With that settled, she closed her eyes and drifted off.

Caroline woke to frantic banging on the kitchen door and opened it to find Dolcie sobbing and incoherent. *What on earth?* Caroline comforted her until she calmed, then gave her a glass of water. She was beyond concerned. Dolcie's clothes were torn, scratches and welts covered her face and hands, and she was obviously dehydrated and exhausted. "Dolcie, what happened? Did someone hurt you?"

Dolcie put her face in her hands and shook her head no. "I can't find Bert."

Confused, Caroline suggested maybe he went fishing or for a walk.

"You don't understand—I've looked everywhere, all night and morning. Bert was gone when I got up to use the bathroom at midnight. There's no trace of him."

"You were out in the wilderness all night, alone? Dolcie, that's beyond dangerous. What were you thinking? Why didn't you call us?"

Dolcie turned red, swollen eyes to Caroline. "Because I thought I could handle it alone like I've been doing. But it's too much now." Her eyes welled up again. "He could be seriously hurt or worse."

Caroline had an inkling but asked the question anyway. "Dolcie, what's going on?"

"Bert was diagnosed with early-onset Alzheimer's a while back. He was in denial, and I wanted to protect his pride, and maintain his dignity, while he was still aware. So, I remained quiet and kept a watchful eye on him. Taking care of him became my way of life, and as the disease progressed, I just dug a little deeper into my reserve. But now..."

Caroline's phone rang, interrupting the conversation. "It's Otis," she said and answered it. "Yes, she is. Okay, I'll tell her and keep her here." Dolcie stood, gripped the island's edge, and braced for the worst. "Otis has Bert, and he's fine. They're on their way." A relieved Dolcie crumpled to the floor.

Caroline called the camp's on-site nurse, and by the time Otis and Bert arrived, Dolcie was revived, vitals checked, and given strict orders to drink plenty of Gatorade, along with a week of bed rest. Bert's demeanor crossed between impatience and confusion until he saw his wife lying on the sofa. He rushed over and sat on the edge of the couch. "Good Lord, Dolores, what happened to your face and hands? And why are you crying?"

She put her hands on his face. "They're happy tears because

you're alright, home safe and sound. I looked for hours and couldn't find you."

"Why would you do that? You know I hunt in the wee hours of Sunday during deer season. Would've got one, too, if this old rifle hadn't jammed. Had one in my sights, pulled the trigger, and nothing." He stuck a thumb towards Otis. "Then this guy came traipsing through the woods and scared the buck off for good."

"I found him in a deer blind in a tree," Otis said.

"Of course you did, son. How else do you hunt?" Bert was losing patience.

"It's not hunting season, Bert," Otis said gently, putting his arm around the older man as Bert's face fell.

Caroline's hand went to her mouth. "My God, he could have killed someone," she whispered. Dolcie gave her head a quick shake and mouthed the word no.

"You sure it's not?" Bert asked. Otis nodded yes. "Damn, Dolores, maybe that doctor wasn't so crazy." Before Dolcie could respond, Teddy and Charlie came running, awake from their nap and ready for action. Teddy asked Bert to play outside, instantly directing Bert's mind from the unthinkable to pleasure. Once he was out of earshot, Dolcie assured Otis and Caroline there was no ammo in the house. She had tried to hide the guns, but Bert was distraught for days, afraid that one of the boys had taken them and could get hurt.

"Sometimes he thinks our boys are still young and live in the house." She closed her eyes, and tears rolled down her cheeks. "I'm just so tired."

"You must be," Caroline said. "I can't believe you've faced this alone."

"Well, she's not the Lone Ranger anymore. We're here, and we'll figure it out together. For now, you and Bert will stay with us so you can get some rest," Otis said.

With her eyes still closed, Dolcie patted his hand, and said, "Okay, Tonto," and fell into a deep sleep.

Otis and Caroline sat on the deck and tried to wrap their heads around everything. It certainly explained Dolcie's odd behavior at times and her mood swings. As they watched Bert play with Teddy, Otis's breath caught. "He's so full of life and energy, the picture of health. How can this be?" It was a rhetorical question; they both knew there was no answer. "Dan and Emmy need to be told. I'll call Dan and have them meet us here once the store closes." Unable to sit and do nothing, he went to find his phone.

Dolcie woke with a jolt, calling for Bert. Caroline ran to assure her he was fine and saw the terror on her face. *My God, she's been the sole caretaker night and day, carrying the heartache and burden on her own. Well, no more,* Caroline silently promised. She managed to get Dolcie to eat some broth before she nodded off again, and as Otis carried her upstairs, Caroline felt her heart crack.

By the time Dan and Emmy arrived, Bert had gone to lie down, making it easier for the couples to talk. Otis brought the Preaces up to date, and Caroline held Emmy as she cried. The four sat in shock and grief, friendship a balm for their pain. They discussed different ways to help the elderly pair who were always there for them. Once Dolcie was well, she could decide what was best. With a plan in place, they were saying goodbye, when a voice asked, "Excuse me, do you know where my fishing gear is?" Bert stood naked at the foot of the stairs, scratching his head. "I can't seem to find it." Otis gently took his arm and led him back upstairs, making a note to put a lock on the guest room door and give Dolcie a key.

This illness would be a monumental challenge, but one they would all face together.

Chapter XXIII

After a week of sleep and care, Dolcie was back to her old self, able to corral the boys, and impatiently waved off any suggestion she should take it easy. Dan, Emmy, Otis, and Caroline had alternated bringing Bert to work with them, but it soon became clear he was beyond that. They needed to talk to Dolcie. Gathered around the kitchen island to share their thoughts, Dolcie spoke first. "Please don't take my boys from me. I'll figure something out, but I need those two little ones." They assured her that was never even considered, and relieved, she was ready to listen.

Otis explained that some of the solutions were already a moot point. They'd thought Bert might come with her to watch the boys or go to work with them but now realized he needed close supervision and redirection to be safe. "So, what's left?" Dolcie asked.

Dan took over. "There's a day center for seniors specializing in dementia near Portland. Emmy and I went to visit and spoke to the director. It's an amazing place, and the people who work there are skilled and caring. It was obviously a passion for them, not just a job. The facility has organized activities for socialization, supervised tasks and music sessions for stimulation, and a namaste room if someone is anxious and needs quiet time."

Dolcie shook her head. "Bert can't be inside all day; he'll never make it." Dan told her about the secured courtyard that provides a place to garden, care for the koi pond, rake, shovel, and even walk a dog on days the staff bring pets.

She wasn't convinced. "Bert will hate it. He's too independent."

Emmy put an arm around her shoulders. "At first, yes, but he can't be left to his own judgment anymore," she said gently.

Dolcie folded into herself. "I know. But how will he get there? I can't drive him in the winter."

"They have a bus for pick up and drop off."

Dolcie was quiet for a time. *This must be so hard for her,* Caroline thought. "Can I go see it for myself?"

"Of course, I'll take you today," Emmy said.

Now came the toughest sell, but that was Caroline's forte. "I've also gotten names of trusted home healthcare workers for you to interview," she said.

"I'll take care of my husband at home. I don't need a stranger milling about our personal space and minding our business." That was the exact reaction they'd expected.

Caroline was ready. "They'd come at bedtime and leave first thing in the morning, so no milling involved and no business to mind. Dolcie, you must take care of yourself to care for Bert and the boys."

"How the hell am I supposed to get a good night's sleep with a stranger in the house?"

"They won't be a stranger once you meet and interview them, and any sleep is better than you get now, which is none."

Unable to argue that she switched gears. "We live on a limited income. We can't afford this daycare, transportation, and overnight care fantasy."

"No, but we can," Otis said. Dolcie immediately went to object, and he held up a hand to stop her. "You are family to us, and family takes care of their own. Period."

Dolcie sat up straighter and raised her chin. "Bert will never allow it; he has too much pride."

Otis softened his voice. "Bert or you? Dolcie, is he even aware of money or finances anymore?"

She shook her head no. Not wanting her husband to suffer due to her pride, she relented. "How can I ever thank you beautiful people enough?"

"One of your shepherd's pies comes to mind," Dan teased.

Emmy gave his arm a playful punch. "You already have; you're the best surrogate grandma to the boys and an earth angel to us all." The rest of them stood and started clapping, making Dolcie blush and almost smile.

Later that evening, when all was quiet, Caroline took the plunge. "I need to go to Boston for a night or two and finalize things. I'd hoped to go in the next week or so, but now, with Bert, I don't know." Caroline saw her husband tense for a split second, and the air between them thickened. He took a deep breath, and it was gone as quickly as it had come.

"Plenty of us to handle things here while you take care of business. Have you told our son?"

"Of course not. I wanted to talk to you first. I hoped we could talk to Teddy together."

Otis gave a sardonic smile Caroline wanted to wipe off his face. "A united front?"

"More like reassurance from both parents. This is the first time either of us has traveled, and he's bound to feel insecure. We need to dispel any worries he has and answer his questions, let him know change isn't something to fear."

Otis gave her a long look as if weighing something in his mind before he spoke. Caroline wanted to ask what but knew to leave well enough alone. "Okay," was all he said.

I guess that went as well as expected, mainly because I held my tongue. Who would've thought I'd be the one to control my reactions, be the voice of reason? She gave herself a mental pat on the back for the effort.

They made love that night, but Caroline felt the distance creeping back in, like an arctic blast seeping through a crack in the door. Determined not to let it blow the door open, she spooned behind her sleeping husband and attempted to ward off the chill.

★ ★ ★

Teddy's initial apprehension faded once they showed him how FaceTime worked, and Caroline promised to call in the morning and before bed while she was away. Otis added the incentive of sleeping in the big bed and fishing. The deal was sealed when Otis assured him Bert and Charlie could go fishing too. "Bye, Mom," he said with a hug. Caroline swore he looked slightly disappointed when she told him she wasn't leaving until next week. She mouthed the words thank you over Teddy's head, and Otis shrugged. Not sure what that meant, Caroline wished a smile had accompanied it. *Baby steps,* she thought and pushed down feelings of annoyance.

Emmy stopped by to fill them in on Dolcie's visit to the center. Reluctant at first, Dolcie warmed to the place as she chatted with the staff, who answered her questions and addressed her concerns. She balked that she couldn't accompany Bert initially to help him adjust. They had to convince her it would prolong his transition and cause him more angst. She turned the corner when another family member shared her experience and what to expect during the first few weeks. Dolcie was thrilled to learn there was a monthly support group and readily took the woman's phone number. Emmy declined

Caroline's offer for tea, whispering that Dan's mood had darkened as she hugged her goodbye.

Dolcie is willing to accept help, Bert needs care, Dan is depressed... More changes, more baby steps. This time, Caroline's sigh escaped.

Chapter XXIV

As expected, Bert hated the center and blamed Dolcie. His behavior towards her alternated between a petulant child and an enraged bully. He'd give her the silent treatment, reject her affection, then rail at her with abusive language the next minute. He would pout and refuse to eat, sometimes knocking the plate to the floor like a toddler, or yell he was hungry and ask why dinner was late when it wasn't. Once, he locked himself in the bathroom and threatened to punch anyone who tried to make him go. At the center, he refused to participate in activities and stood by the door all day asking when his ride home would arrive.

The staff assured Dolcie this was typical and he would adjust. Her support friend knew the different emotions Dolcie was battling and called every night to listen with a sympathetic ear. She offered her own stories to let Dolcie see she was not alone, and as bad as the situation felt, it would pass. Oddly enough, Bert didn't mind the home healthcare worker. No one could figure out why but all were grateful for the one transition going smoothly.

Dolcie appreciated the experienced advice and suggestions from the support group but knew the real reason she could hold it together was the Preaces and Addisens. Caring for the boys and the unconditional, pure love they sprinkled in the air kept her going and her heart from breaking, like magic fairy dust. Emmy, Dan, Otis, and Caroline watched closely and were there when Dolcie needed a break or Bert needed a distraction. The couple's adopted family was the glue that kept their shattered life from splintering into irretrievable pieces.

★   ★   ★

With things so unsettled, Caroline contemplated postponing her trip. But appointments were in place, and canceling a first meeting would likely be a death knell. Always the voice of sensibility, Emmy mentioned this wouldn't be the last time life took a turn at an inopportune time, that there were enough of them to manage, and it was only for a short time. She was right, of course, and Caroline gave her friend an appreciative look. Having plowed through the ups and downs alone for most of her adult life, she was always struck by the security and sense of belonging community offered. *What a gift it is to have a tribe to share life's joys and burdens,* she thought, not for the first time.

Caroline decided to take the train to Boston and use the ride to finalize her closing presentations. She was confident in her corporate pitch due to her years at PG&G but was afraid of overdoing it with residential clients. To sell across a coffee table required a much different approach than a conference room. Caroline reviewed the pricing structure she and Emmy had agreed upon and, satisfied, closed her eyes and gave in to the hypnotizing motion of the train.

Caroline arrived in the city, refreshed and ready to work. After checking into the hotel, she went straight to the Morris project. Almost complete, it was breathtaking, with Emmy's signature design written all over it. Wisteria cascaded over a gated archway that opened into an oasis of colorful tranquility.

Stone walls defined tiered flower gardens as if wrapping them in protective arms, and under a pergola, a river stone fountain trickled into a koi pond dressed in lily pads and water plants. A framed porch swing and wicker patio chairs were strategically placed to provide shade or sun, and young climbing roses reached for trellises that awaited their arrival. Two old oak trees towered above, reminiscent of grandparents looking proudly over their clan. Caroline took pictures and knew the images alone would sell Cardinal Designs. *Emmy, you are one talented visionary lady,* she thought fondly. Five years in business and Emmy's artistry still amazed Caroline.

Armed with her photographic weapon, Caroline left for her first interview, sure of success. However, by the third appointment, she noticed a trend. All three clients were impressed and promised to contact Cardinal in the spring, but from years of experience, Caroline knew a signed contract was the only guarantee.

Over a quick salad for lunch, she came up with a plan. Cardinal would offer a discounted rate for fall cleanup and 20% off the fall planting if they signed on for a garden design in the spring/summer. Caroline gave her water glass a celebratory raise and started drawing up a revised contract on a napkin. Suddenly she stopped mid-scribble and smacked her head. *I can't believe I almost did it again. I need to run this by Emmy first.* She put the pen down and called her partner.

Caroline explained the situation and her solution to Emmy, who was on board but had a suggestion. "Why don't you concentrate on clients and forget about hiring until spring. If you land enough contracts, have the crew stay until the end of October, and we'll take care of the fall up here. That'll save some money."

"Don't forget the Addisen temporary help goes back to school the week before Labor Day."

"They'll still be available on weekends," Emmy countered.

"What if the crew doesn't agree to stay down here?"

"Then we hire early and cut our losses. But my money's on your persuasive skills convincing them."

Caroline laughed. "Challenge accepted."

"Oh, and one more thought," Emmy added. "Why not add a non-refundable deposit on the contract as a safety net?"

"Great idea. I think I'm wearing off on you."

"Yep. Heaven help us all," Emmy deadpanned and hung up.

By the end of the second day, Caroline had signed over a dozen residential accounts and two of the three corporate accounts. *Not too shabby for two days' work. You've still got it, McMerritt.* But Caroline had to persuade the crew to stay through October before she could celebrate in earnest.

Boston's North End offered some of the best Italian food this side of Italy and was close enough to make the last train out of North Station. She called and asked the foreman to meet her for dinner, his choice of restaurant. Being Sicilian, he chose Giacomo's on Hanover Street. His favorite food, a top-notch restaurant, and her negotiation abilities nailed it. It took some bargaining; more money, some guys able to go home to wives who'd run out of patience, and the okay to hire replacements of his choice. They closed the deal over tiramisu.

Once settled on the train, Caroline called Emmy, but it went to voice mail. Tired, she was relieved and left a message; all was good, and they'd talk tomorrow.

It was after midnight when Caroline got home. She tiptoed into the master suite and found her whole heart sleeping in the bed. Teddy was curled up between Otis and Charlie, fully protected and unconditionally loved. She climbed into her son's bed and fell into a deep sleep with that vision's warmth in her bones and the faint smell of her young son on the pillow.

Chapter XXV

"Mommy's home!" Teddy yelled and jumped on the bed. Between Teddy's kisses and Charlie's licks, Caroline's face was soaked with slobber before she was fully awake.

"What a wonderful welcome home," she exclaimed inside a ball of arms, legs, fur, and giggles. She saw Otis in the doorway, and wished he'd join in the fun.

"You were missed," he said, with a smile that didn't make it to his eyes. *Is he intentionally cold, or am I oversensitive?* Before she could ask if that included him, Otis announced it was time to make breakfast, and left the happy scene. Caroline refused to let it ruin her homecoming, shook it off, and herded her flock to the kitchen.

At breakfast, Teddy talked non-stop about his adventures in her absence, which left no room for conversation between his parents. Caroline wondered if Otis was as relieved as she was. Excited to share the Boston news with Emmy, she still took a walk with Teddy. More effective than any drug, a dose of her son and nature was an elixir that eased her lingering thoughts of Otis's chilly welcome home.

Caroline got to work and found her partner staring out the window, lost in thought. "Emmy, is everything okay? Talk to me," she said, pulling up a chair.

"Later. Right now, I want to hear all about your trip."

Caroline filled her in, including every detail, and watched Emmy's face brighten as the story unfolded. "Wow, this is really happening."

Caroline assured her it certainly was, and this was only the first round of marketing. "I plan to keep at it all year, just as successfully. We'll need the nursery up and running for next spring."

Caroline's enthusiasm was contagious, and Emmy was over the moon at the thought of her nursery so close, but couldn't quell a niggling feeling of apprehension. Where would they get the money? The land? Caroline pointed out Addisens owned plenty of undeveloped land, and Cardinal Design could apply for a business loan. If the bank wanted more collateral, she would ask Otis to co-sign. Emmy wasn't convinced. "Have you talked to Otis about this?"

"Not yet, but I'm sure he'll give us the land." *Co-signing is a different story, but I'll figure it out,* she added to herself.

"I'm not worried about that. My concern is how Otis responds to Cardinal's rapid growth and all it entails," Emmy said. Caroline reminded her Otis agreed to give her a year. "Doesn't mean he figured on so much so soon," Emmy countered.

"You let me worry about Otis," Caroline said more confidently than she felt. "Now, what's going on with you? Is it Dan?"

Emmy confirmed it was, and she was beyond worried. "It's worse than previous years. He'd always get down and reflect around his mother's death anniversary but rebounded after a few days to grieve. He can't rally this time; if anything, he's getting worse. Dan puts a game face on for others, but at home he's withdrawn and despondent; he says it's exhausting to pretend all day, and he needs to be real at home." Emmy's eyes filled. "Even Caleb can't pull him back. I try to talk to him, but Dan swears he doesn't know what is wrong. And that terrifies me."

Caroline put an arm around her friend and handed her a tissue. "Sounds like depression to me."

"But why? We have a good life, the one we always dreamed of." Emmy's face contorted. "Oh my God, you don't think he wants out, do you? Maybe he's fallen out of love with me, and—"

Caroline cut her off. "No way, Emmy. Dan adores you and Caleb." Caroline took a moment to organize her thoughts and then shared them with her friend. "Dan's mother was his age when she took her life. It was situational, but what if there was an underlying issue? Depression is an illness that can manifest at any age for seemingly no reason, and it can be hereditary. Maybe Dan was genetically inclined, and his age and the anniversary triggered it." She paused, then added, "I'm no doctor and could be way off, but it's worthwhile to check his family history and research the disease."

Emmy didn't know whether to be more concerned or relieved, but either way, what Caroline said made sense. "Thanks for listening, and the insight," she said, dabbing her eyes. "You always know how to find a path forward."

"It comes from years of crisis management to avoid death by competitive backstab."

The friends shared a laugh, and the air seemed lighter. Feeling better, Emmy suggested the four of them have dinner, and they could bring the guys up to speed together. Caroline, grateful for the support, readily agreed. "You're not so bad at thinking ahead yourself," she said.

"I've learned from the best," Emmy said. "A three-to-one ratio will be tough for Otis to beat back."

A united front, Caroline thought, the irony not lost on her.

That evening, Caroline watched Dan closely, and Emmy was right: he had a great game face. As close as they were, she saw no sign of the turmoil inside him. In fact, it was Dan who opened the conversation about Cardinal. "Okay, you two, spill it. Emmy has walked on a cloud all day because of exciting news, but I had to wait until dinner to hear. It's dinner, so let's have it." Caroline went from beginning to end and became more animated as the trip's story unfolded. Dan beamed throughout and asked questions, while Otis sat with a forced smile and didn't engage. She ended with her marketing strategy and goals for the remainder of the fiscal year, then turned the floor over to a barely contained Emmy.

Blushing with pride, Emmy showed the pictures of the Morris project and shared their plan for a nursery and office complex. "We'll need the nursery built and stocked by spring. Can you believe it? My dream a reality."

Dan scooped her up and swung her around. "You bet I can. With your creative artistry and Caroline's business savvy, I knew it would happen." He winked at Caroline, "We always believed." He pulled Caroline to her feet and hugged her tight. Otis remained stoic and watched the celebration unfold.

"Congratulations," he finally said. "It's really taking off at a breakneck pace."

"Of course it is. Have you met your wife? Tenacious and charming."

"That she is," Otis conceded and raised his beer bottle in Caroline's direction. "Have you ladies already decided where?" Otis held his wife's stare. *You sarcastic prick* was on the tip of her tongue.

Emmy sensed danger and stepped in. "That's kind of up to you. We hoped to keep it in Addisen but can move if necessary." *Well played, Em.*

That, coming from Emmy, seemed to register something

within Otis. "Of course, we'll build it on Addisen land. I only meant whereabouts." *Did you? Really?*

The four of them looked over a map of Addisen's undeveloped land. They chose a location away from the lake and recreation area but not too far from town. Dan suggested they hire a contractor to clear the land and break ground this summer and have the concrete poured by early September. After Labor Day, he and Otis could take over construction.

"We're talking about a costly expansion based on a gamble," Otis pointed out. *No, based on my ability to deliver.* Caroline laid out the preliminary numbers she'd worked up and their intention to secure a bank loan. "You'll need a lot of collateral for a note that big. Does the company have it?"

"No," Caroline conceded. "But if I can't persuade them to take the chance, I'll come up with it."

"How?" *He knows damn well how.*

Caroline bristled; she would not beg. "Investors."

Otis raised his eyebrows and grinned. *Smirked?* "Looks like we're building a nursery, Dan."

Chapter XXVI

Caroline saw the Preaces out and turned to her husband, anger setting her green eyes afire. "What the hell was that?"

"What the hell was what?" Otis asked calmly, infuriating her even more.

"You know exactly what I'm talking about."

"No, but I'm sure you're about to enlighten me."

"The disengaged attitude and your nonchalance while the rest of us celebrated. Your obnoxious response when Dan complimented me. The challenging tone you took about the location, knowing full well we expected to build on Addisen land. And you called the whole thing a gamble. Thanks for your faith in my ability to deliver. Oh, and the money; I felt like a mouse being batted around by a cat before the kill."

She watched as Otis drummed his fingers on the island, aware it was how he counted to ten to check his temper. Still, when he spoke, it was strained. "Ever think that it was surprise and hurt that fueled my reaction? I was the only one not in the know, and my wife took the trip. It pissed me off. And the land? All you had to do was ask. But you didn't. You cut me out. And Caroline, it *is* a gamble. That was an observation, not a dig at you."

"Not in the know? When was I supposed to bring you up

to date? Otis, you weren't exactly warm and fuzzy towards me this morning, and you took off before Teddy was through his stories."

Otis ran a hand across his face. "This is more complicated than I thought it would be."

Caroline plopped down on a stool and agreed. "Change isn't easy; we just have to get a little better at it."

Otis was quiet for a long while. "Or stay status quo."

"Not an option," Caroline said. And this time, it was she who left the room. *Time to journal, not speak.*

What. The. Fuck. Status quo? Has he listened to anything I've said? Of course, he has. He just doesn't like what he hears. Otis has never shied away from change. In fact, he usually initiates it and meets it head on with optimism and confidence. Our marriage, fatherhood, improvements to Addisen, anything. The difference is he sees those as positives and this as a negative, and that alters his attitude. Which, in turn, makes me defensive. 'Round and 'round we go... I don't know how to fix it. I feel like I'm banging my head against the wall.

Why can't he trust me? Why does he refuse to see how important this is to me? Or does he see but cares more about what he wants? Why can't he support me as I have him? Is he threatened by the idea of my success, or am I reading him all wrong?

My frustration morphed into anger tonight, and I can't allow that to continue. I need to maintain my equilibrium to make Otis see this change is uncomfortable but positive. I'll no longer think of it as beating my head against the wall but as beating my heart against my husband's. Hopefully, that helps keep my temper in check and my patience abundant.

Caroline closed the journal, started to call Will, and stopped. From the time she could remember, her brother was her go-to guy. But this time? Her gut said no. Will was in the throes of Otis's side of change, not hers. Caroline's intuition told her to leave it alone or risk a second confrontation, and she wasn't up for another letdown tonight. She hoped Hector was with Will, and Emmy and Dan were resolving their issues, which left only her own counsel. Tired of thinking, Caroline opened a novel and lost herself in someone else's world for a break.

★ ★ ★

Dolcie called the next morning and needed the day off; she wasn't feeling well. Concerned, Caroline drove over and found she looked as bad as she'd sounded. Dolcie assured her a doctor wasn't necessary but couldn't bring herself to explain the problem. Instead, she played a recording from the nanny cam installed in the bedroom for Bert's safety. What Caroline saw and heard was heart-wrenching and a testament to love.

"Dolores, are you awake?" Caroline could hear Bert's tears and the pain in his voice.

"What's wrong, dear?" Dolcie reached for the bedside lamp, but Bert asked her to leave it dark and took her hand.

"I'm so scared," he whimpered.

Dolcie put her arms around him and pulled him close. "I am too. But like all the storms we've had in life, we will navigate this together," she soothed.

Bert sobbed. "But I won't be here for you. I'm fading, and soon I'll be lost."

Dolcie sat up, turned on the light, took his face in her hands, and looked deep into his eyes. "You will always be here, in my heart, and never lost; I will be right beside you as you walk towards the light."

He pulled her to him and kissed her passionately, like when they were young. "I love you, woman."

"And I you, husband." Dolcie shut off the lamp, and Bert lay his head on her chest while she stroked his hair like a child.

"Dolores?"

"Hmmm?"

"Please don't ever put me in a home," he pleaded. His wife promised she would never.

"I'm so sorry to put you through this," he said, falling asleep. When his breathing told Dolcie he was safely asleep, she let her tears flow.

"This morning, he asked me who I was and refused breakfast, insisting he'd already eaten. Don't ask me how, but I know last night was my husband's last moment of clarity; his mind is now fully entombed in its diseased state. It'll be harder for me but easier for him, don't you think?"

In awe, Caroline could only nod. "My God, Dolcie, you are so strong."

The elderly woman shrugged. "What choice do I have? He was a solid, honest man, a loving husband, and a great father. It wasn't all rainbows and unicorns, but we had a good life. I wouldn't change a thing about our years past."

"Because you always loved one another."

Dolcie gave a wistful smile. "Most days." She patted Caroline's hand. "Now, let me get some sleep before he comes home from the center."

Caroline was surprised but comforted by Dolcie's answer. If a lifelong love had weathered days of doubt, surely the rest of them would be okay.

Chapter XXVII

Caroline called the store and brought Emmy up to date on Dolcie. "That poor woman," Emmy said. "It's worse for her than him now." Caroline agreed but reminded her Dolcie would survive, but Bert would not. "You're right, but I doubt that provides her much solace." They each wanted to share their evening events, but both husbands were within earshot, so it would have to wait.

Caroline put on a movie to occupy the boys and sat at Otis's desk to work on Boston. After lunch, Caleb and Teddy made their nanny get-well cards while Caroline prepared dinner for all, then called to check on Dolcie. Glad to hear her sounding better, she phoned Emmy and suggested the families dine together, partly for convenience but mostly to avoid an awkward night with Otis. Caroline could tell by Emmy's despondent tone that things hadn't gone smoothly at the Preace household the night before either.

Dinner was relaxed, mainly because Caleb and Teddy were there and monopolized the conversation. But things took a rapid turn for the worse once they went to play. Dan clapped his hands. "Okay, let's talk logistics on the nursery. The clock's ticking, and we should be ready in case winter comes early." Emmy mentioned it was only August and was gifted with an icy stare.

"I'd love to, Dan, but every time I have an opinion or suggestion, my wife accuses me of sabotaging her or worse."

Caroline had braced for a wisecrack, but the bluntness of Otis's comment hit a nerve. "Seriously, Otis?"

Dan spoke. "You're lucky, buddy. My wife thinks I'm fucking crazy."

"Dan!" Emmy was mortified. "I said depressed; that's not the same as crazy." Dan went to reply when Charlie barked, and they turned to see two frightened little boys, eyes wide, frozen in the doorway.

Caroline recovered first. "It's okay, guys. We're play-acting like you do with Dolcie and the puppets." She was pretty sure not even the dog bought it, but the other adults backed her, and make-your-own sundaes worked wonders as a distraction for the boys. Caroline silently vowed that this would never happen again and longed to talk to her journal.

What the hell is happening to us? We're so touchy, ready to do battle at the slightest provocation, unable to accept suggestions or constructive criticism. How are we supposed to compromise and welcome our different opinions and insights if we no longer see them coming from a place of love but an enemy camp? Will and Hector, Dan and Emmy, and Otis and I had solid relationships, secure in the trusted acceptance of our partners and our oneness, no matter what. The three marriages have lost that unconditional acceptance and sense of wholeness. Instead, we feel we must prove ourselves and justify our feelings and stance. Inevitably every relationship goes through rough patches and changes over time, and adjustments are needed. Why are we finding it so difficult?

Maybe I was wrong to think we could maneuver through marriage's challenges as Dolcie and my parents' generation had. It was a different time, less difficult, and more basic. Life has obstacles and complications now, making us more complex as individuals and couples. Or is it we are spoiled and self-involved?

Whatever the reason, we need to figure out the best solution for our situations quickly. Resentment is an emotional staph infection that devours intimacy and kills love at its core.

Dolcie arrived the next morning to find Emmy and Caroline hunched over mugs of coffee, looking defeated. "You two look like you just lost the Big Game."

"I'm afraid we're in the process of doing just that," Emmy said.

Dolcie poured herself a cup and sat down. "Okay, let's have it." Each woman filled her in on their story, and Caroline added her thoughts on how marriage was harder to navigate in today's world. "Bullshit," Dolcie stated, making Emmy choke on a sip of coffee. "You don't think we had issues, problems, hard feelings? The difference is we never saw quitting as an option. We'd made a commitment and had families and homes. So what if we weren't blissfully content with one another at times? We kept our eye on the prize and found a way forward. And it was the women who figured out how to do it."

Dolcie continued, "Men see themselves as providers, protectors, strong beings that keep all harm from their loved ones, king of the jungle. It's out of their control, something embedded in them with the Y chromosome." She looked at Emmy.

"They take offense when perceived weaknesses are pointed out." Then at Caroline. "Or no longer feel they're enough, their manhood challenged. It embarrasses them, makes them feel inadequate."

"But none of that is true," Emmy said. "We don't feel that way at all."

"Doesn't matter. That's the way they see it. I don't care how evolved a man is; if he feels a woman's strength surpassing his, he'll feel threatened."

"So, what do we do?" Caroline asked.

"You find what works best for your circumstance and fix it. It'll take a few stumbles until you hit your stride, but you're smart, capable ladies; you'll figure it out. Now pick your chins up off the floor and get to work. I have two boys to tend to."

Dolcie was back.

Emmy and Caroline discussed Dolcie's observations. It all made sense. It was the first time a partner ever felt threatened and challenged in the three marriages. Justified or not, their feelings were real and had to be dealt with diplomatically. Fair? Maybe not, but Dolcie made some excellent points. The friends realized, like Hector, they would have to come up with a solution on their own. Emmy expressed concerns about manipulation, but Caroline reminded her of the alternative. Dan required professional help to live a healthy life or risk his mother's fate. Caroline needed to be whole to thrive as a wife and mother. Wisely, they decided to follow the elder woman's sound advice.

Chapter XXVIII

The remainder of summer and early fall flew by like a New York minute. Along with the usual summer chaos, constructing the nursery kept everyone busy. After more back and forth with Otis over trips, Caroline took Will's tact and chose silence over words for a while. She let Otis's snide remarks dissipate into empty air and ignored his sullen moods until he eventually stopped. Not optimal, but more peaceful. The distance between them widened considerably, but Caroline preferred it to more resentment. She had no idea where Otis's head was and knew it was not a long-term solution, but for now, it worked. Emmy, occupied with the nursery, hadn't mentioned Dan, so Caroline assumed she also had found a temporary fix.

In late September, Will and Hector came up to help Otis and Dan finish the nursery. Caroline was ecstatic and a little envious to see the closeness returned to their body language. Will talked freely about time spent with Cameron, Joel, and Miguel and even admitted he'd recently enjoyed a weekend in the city. Caroline cornered Hector the first chance she got. "Spill it, brother-in-law. How did you get him to turn around so quickly?"

"I didn't," Hector said. "The two of us looked at facts and chose light over dark."

"Clarify, please," Caroline requested, and Hector did. After seeing Will hit it off with his friends on the Fourth of July, he realized it was a matter of Will's stubbornness and aversion to change, not some major issue that Hector imagined. Will saw the friends were decent, kind people, not some party animals out to make a statement.

"That was it?"

Hector laughed. "Hell no, but it opened the door." The couple shared long talks, reviewed and evaluated their life together, and what each wanted for the future. It was clear to both that what they had was unique, and neither relished an existence without the other. "That meant Will needed to accept our life was expanding, and he had to adapt and grow with it. And I had to let go of resentments and quit finding attitude, his and mine."

"Have you?"

"It's a work in progress. But we're now on the same course, working towards a mutual goal and determined to make it." Caroline hoped she and Otis would find their path soon and avoid the fork in the road now within sight.

★   ★   ★

Once the nursery was finished, Hector returned to board meetings and his coffee shop while Will stayed to help Caroline move the office and showroom from cabin to nursery. Emmy was knee-deep in potting soil, surrounded by shrubs and bushes, her head in a colorful cloud of seedlings and perennials; Caroline hadn't seen her friend this excited since the birth of Caleb. Dan's part-timer had quit, and Otis needed to winterize the rentals, so brother and sister were on their own, not that Caroline minded. *It will give us a chance to catch up and repair our frayed bond.* She still felt the sting of Will's angry words and intuited a guarded vibe from him towards her. There was a film of uneasiness between them that Caroline wanted cleared. Before she could broach the subject, Will beat her to it.

"I was out of line that day in the driveway, and I'm sorry. I couldn't handle it when you disagreed and took a different side."

"I didn't choose sides; I tried to help like you always do for me. Unfortunately, my delivery doesn't possess your finesse."

"Or maybe I couldn't deal with my kid sister seeing me less than a brilliant hero."

"Brilliant?" Caroline teased.

"Okay, profound. Are we good?"

Caroline gave his arm a playful punch. "Yep. Now quit slacking off, we have a job to do."

While the duo worked, Caroline expressed her happiness at his marriage's progress and lamented on the discourse in her own. Will asked her to elaborate on what she saw as the biggest issue, and she answered immediately. "Otis doesn't support me. He said he would give it a year but bucks me over the simplest things. My short trips to Boston, working late on occasion at home. And he withholds his affection in retaliation, keeps his distance."

"He's funded Cardinal's expansion and busted his ass to build the nursery complex. Seems to me that's the ultimate show of support. Have you acknowledged it?" Caroline's silence was his answer. "Maybe he's focused on the small things because you haven't expressed appreciation for the important ones. And he hasn't retreated emotionally out of spite but hurt."

Once again, Will rights my course. "That's a great observation, brother."

"Some might even say brilliant," Will quipped. Caroline rolled her eyes, and he smiled, both comfortable back in the roles they were born into.

★ ★ ★

That evening, as she and Otis read in the library, a feeling of shyness settled over Caroline as she approached her husband. "Otis?" He looked up from his book and waited. "I've been fixated on the small stuff between us and never told you how much I appreciate that you backed Cardinal's growth. I know it's not what you want, yet you've put in a lot of time and money to make it happen, and I've never said thank you. So, thank you."

Otis raised his eyebrows in surprise. "You're welcome," he said and closed his book. "We should talk."

The couple spoke of hard feelings each fostered and discovered how resentment had misconstrued intent on both sides. The conclusion was silence, which, while less combative, was more harmful and not the way to resolve issues. They agreed to hold their tongues within earshot of Teddy, but never overnight. Things would be hashed out in the mancave, with Teddy asleep in his bed. "We were never ones to hold back, and it was a mistake to start now," Otis said.

"Speak for yourself. I have always been the epitome of restraint and emotional control," Caroline deadpanned.

Otis laughed. "I stand corrected, milady." With things lighter between them, he felt comfortable enough to add, "Now, may I escort you to the marital bed?"

Contoured against her husband after making love, Caroline registered why she had felt shy; as an adult, she'd never sincerely apologized to a man for anything. She wasn't sure how to go about it and afraid of Otis's rejection. Instead, he responded with a willingness to set down a different path. *No fork in the road for us yet. Thank you, spirit, for guiding us through,* she thought and drifted off to sleep.

Chapter XXIX

Before Caroline knew it, fall was a memory, and Christmas was coming fast. Her acknowledgment of Otis's contributions helped eliminate a lot of the snark between them, but they still clashed at times. True to their word, they'd argue through it in the mancave, and mornings were now a fresh start instead of an anger hangover. Will was right to point out her failure to show appreciation, and she was correct that communication lines had to stay open. Silence is not an option to sustain a relationship. *I'll be sure to tell him we each had sound ideas.*

She smiled at the thought as she poured a mug of coffee and stared at the breathtaking masterpiece the lakefront windows framed. Mother Nature had covered Addisen in a magnificent down comforter of white the night before. It was still pristine, unscathed at this early hour but for the forest residents who journeyed out after the storm. Caroline bundled up and stepped onto the deck to join them. She watched a small herd of deer gather to nibble on snow-covered saplings and spotted a family of coyotes roaming the tree line. A hawk glided gracefully through the cold gray dawn, and a fox comically stuck its head in and out of a tree hollow, not sure it wanted to venture out. All this life took place within a cocoon of hushed quietude unique to a snow-covered forest. The only sound was tree limbs groaning under the added weight and the whisper of the wind as it danced through the pines and over the lake.

Frozen, Caroline cleared the bird feeders and took one final breath of purity before going inside. Soon, Addisen's two-legged creatures would awaken and celebrate the overnight gift with snowmobiles, ice fishing, skiing, skating, sledding, and bonfires; the stillness replaced with children's laughter and dozens of shovels scraping snow off the lake. Caroline raised her mug and blew a kiss to the cardinal who'd landed on the feeder and went to warm up in front of the fire.

Otis insisted on going to get Dolcie, much to her chagrin. Snowshoes or not, 18 inches of snow was a challenge, even for her. She groused about being treated like an old woman but brightened when Teddy told her his plans for the day. "You, me, and Caleb are gonna build a fort, make a snowman, go sledding, drink tons of cocoa with marshmallows, and make snow angels."

"Is that all?" Dolcie asked.

"Nope. Then we'll do it all over again."

"Well, at least somebody around here sees I'm not ready to be put out to pasture," Dolcie said, shooting Otis a look.

Otis gave her a wink and kissed the top of her head. "I take care of the people I love, whether they like it or not," he said and left to plow before she scolded him further.

Dan dropped off Emmy and Caleb and went to help Otis plow. Caroline sensed something was off with Emmy and suggested they go cross-country skiing for some fresh air. "We can't go to work until the roads are clear anyway," she reasoned. Dolcie, eager to start her day with the boys, shooed the women out the door. Caroline expected to go at a leisurely pace, but Emmy took off with a vengeance. *Yep,* Caroline thought, *she's got steam to let off* and gave her friend some space. When she finally caught up, she found Emmy, hands on her knees, breathing hard. "I really needed that," she panted.

Once her breathing steadied, the pair continued skiing at a conversational gait. Caroline knew Emmy wanted to talk and waited patiently until she was ready. "I snapped last night," she finally said. Caroline assured her while it wasn't the norm for her, most people did so on occasion. "No. I mean, I snapped. Like a rubber band that's pulled taut for too long."

"Are you okay?"

"That's just the thing, yes. Yes, I am. And I'm afraid that doesn't bode well for my marriage."

Oh shit... "What happened?"

Emmy, calmly (too calmly), related the story. She and Caleb were baking sugar cookies and singing "Jingle Bells," and Dan was on the couch watching the game. He turned the volume up to drown out their singing. Innocently, Caleb sang louder, then the TV got louder until Dan swore, shut it off, and stormed into the bedroom, slamming the door. Caleb went silent, and tears started to fall down his cheeks. "Mommy, why doesn't Daddy like us anymore?" Emmy had to scoop him into her lap and rock him to soothe his broken heart. She tried to explain Daddy was sick, and it made him act funny sometimes. "Why doesn't he go to the doctor's and get better?"

"And that's when it happened, Caroline. I had no answer for my little boy. There wasn't one." Emmy had tried to reset the festive mood but failed and put her son to bed sad, with bruised feelings, a week before Christmas. She entered their bedroom without knocking and turned on the overhead light. "Dan sat up to confront me but stopped when he saw my face. I told him verbatim what Caleb had said and how his behavior affected me. I informed him I would no longer tolerate his moods or allow his pride and stubbornness to scar our son. I had treaded softly around him for months, but no more.

Caleb and I would leave after Christmas if he didn't agree to get help."

"Oh my God, what did he do?" Caroline couldn't believe what she was hearing.

"He started to sob, and I was numb to it. The man I have loved since childhood had a meltdown, and I did nothing to comfort him. Instead, I pushed forward and asked if he wanted his son to suffer as he had, to grow up without a parent. Because even though he was alive, he was now absent from Caleb's life. Did he think that was any less painful than death for their son? And what if he became as hopeless as his mother? What then? Caleb would be old enough to remember the devastating act." Emmy let out a ragged breath.

"I never dreamed I could love anyone more than Dan, but I do. I will shield Caleb from harm, even if it's his flesh and blood, and at a great loss to me."

"Oh, Emmy. I'm so sorry it's come to this. I'd hoped it had gotten better."

"Me too. But either way, it will now be resolved."

Chapter XXX

I have to do something. I can't just sit back and watch this happen, Caroline thought. *But what?* She was curled up in the library, wrapped in her mom's favorite afghan, attempting to ward off the chill that radiated from within. Dan and Emmy, no more? It was unfathomable. Caroline knew the couple had endured trouble in the past, but this was different. She saw the resolve in Emmy's eyes and heard the conviction in her voice. Emmy was a mama bear determined to protect her cub; not even Dan would be spared if he posed a threat to Caleb's well-being. *Think, woman, there must be a way to get through to Dan.* The cardinal landed on the sill, and Caroline remembered her mother's journal. "Thanks, Mom," she said and began to mark passages in the diary.

The following morning Caroline surprised Dan at the store. He got right down to business. "I suppose Emmy told you she's going to leave me," he said flatly.

"No. What I heard was a wife and mother, frustrated, concerned, and out of options. But you, Dan, have options. If your marriage does end, it's because you checked out months ago and refused her help. Think about all you'll lose before you dig further in and fuck it up."

Caroline sat the worn book on the counter and answered

Dan's puzzled look. "My mother's journal; I believe you'll find the marked entries enlightening. She helped you to understand as a teenager; perhaps her words can reach you as a man."

Caroline left without another word. *Okay, Mom, work your magic,* she prayed and crossed her fingers inside her coat pockets.

★　★　★

Christmas was a week away, and Caroline was in a conundrum. She and Otis traditionally hosted Christmas Day, but everything was askew this year. Dan and Emmy were a mess, and controlling tension in her own marriage was a full-time job. Would her late invite stir the pot if Will and Hector had already made plans with friends? Bert's disease had progressed, and their sons and family intended to come for the holidays. Would they prefer a private family day? In the end, Caroline decided if there was ever a time they all needed one another, it was now. She sat down and made the calls.

Her first call was to Will, who readily agreed and asked to invite Joel, Cameron, and Miguel. "They enjoyed the Fourth and would love Addisen's Christmas Eve. We can stay in Mom and Dad's cabin." Caroline loved the idea and was excited that Will had suggested it. *I guess they are no longer just Hector's friends.* Dolcie was thrilled at the prospect of her two families together for Christmas and couldn't wait to coordinate the menu with Otis. Caroline made a note to give Otis a heads-up about his new sous-chef.

Her last call was to Emmy. "Things are so bad, and there's no telling how Christmas morning will go. I don't think we'd add much to the celebration." *No way the Preaces aren't coming.*

Caroline had an idea. "After the Christmas Eve festivities,

you guys come here for the night. Teddy and Caleb can hang their stockings, leave cookies, milk, and carrots under the tree, and share all the traditions. Guaranteed those two little boys will have the best Christmas ever."

"What if Dan won't agree?"

"He'll come. Remember the game face he puts on around others? If he doesn't show, the truth will." Caroline heard Emmy sniffle. "You okay?"

"Better than okay, and grateful for you. You just saved our Christmas." *My goal is to save more than that, my friend.*

Dolcie and Otis conspired to keep the menu secret and promised a feast fit for kings. Caroline prepared her parents' cabin for Will and company, decorating a tree and hanging a stocking for each on the mantle. Emmy kept two over-stimulated preschoolers from imploding by writing letters to Santa and making Christmas cards for everyone, and Charlie pranced around like a puppy. Even Dan was whistling "Jingle Bells" and teaching Caleb and Teddy the names of Santa's reindeer. Caroline's leap of faith had brightened everyone's holiday mood.

On December 23, a Cherokee Jeep with Connecticut plates roared into town, loaded with holiday cheer and five kids disguised as male adults in Santa hats. After a round of hugs and back-slapping, all went their separate ways to rest up for Addisen's Christmas Eve festivities. Hector said they should lie low for the day and recover from the NYC Christmas frenzy before taking on Addisen's cheer. The Addisen group loved the idea since they were exhausted from the long week of preparation.

The following morning, as they all gathered for Otis's famous pancakes, Joel asked what to expect for the town's celebration. "Will and Hector are very secretive about it. They say words can't do it justice." Everyone nodded in agreement and chose to let them experience it for themselves. Cameron joked that he hadn't brought his tuxedo, and Caroline assured him he'd need something much warmer and less formal.

With everyone's bellies full, Otis announced it was time to get to work, and while the guys donned cold weather gear, Joel asked what they were going to do. "You'll see," Otis said, tossing him a ski mask.

"Looks like we're about to rob a bank," Miguel quipped.

"Except there's no bank in sight," Cameron reasoned. "And snowshoes don't make for a quick getaway." Laughing, Otis gathered up his city elves and led them on their adventure while Emmy and Caroline started their preparations for the evening.

At 3:00, people gathered at the camp's lakeside, with skates and children in tow, and soon the air was dense with heartfelt greetings and sounds of children at play. Bonfires were lit for warmth, and the smell of burning wood mingled with pine and woolen mittens, as Christmas songs played through out-door speakers. In true Addisen fashion, the main bunkhouse was lined with tables of homemade cookies and sweets, each platter with recipe copies to share. The intoxicating aroma of cinnamon and nutmeg, intertwined with hot apple cider and cocoa, created the epitome of Christmas's scent. The elderly, happy to be out of the cold, donned elf hats and served merriment and cheer along with the goodies.

Caleb and Teddy were each allowed to open an early present, a pair of double-bladed skates, and their dads gave them their first lesson. Later, warming by the fire, Dan and Otis boasted that their sons were naturals, good enough to skate for the Boston Bruins one day.

At dusk, everyone congregated around the fires, held hands, and the Unitarian minister led a prayer of thanks. As they began to sing "Silent Night," a life-sized nativity scene became bathed in a serene radiance, and girls dressed as angels adorned with white lights glided on the ice as surrounding trees burst into a rainbow of colored lights.

The caroling continued as the night stars brightened, a heavenly gift from above. The city elves, wonderstruck, now understood there were no words. This event, a happening, evoked a sensation that engaged and tantalized all five senses at once and set one's center aglow. It was a spiritual experience, a true Addisen blessing.

Chapter XXXI

Caroline wasn't the only one up at dawn on Christmas morning. Caleb, Teddy, and Charlie almost beat her. She sent them to wake the rest before they raced down to the tree. Amid a shower of wrapping paper and cascading ribbons, shouts of "This is just what I wanted!" and "Teddy, look!" and "Santa, thank you!" mixed with enthusiastic barking and parents' claps of joy. Emmy mouthed "thank you" to her friend, and Caroline formed a heart with her hands. Gift opening was over in a flash, and while the moms tried to organize the chaos, their sons kept pulling things back out. Laughing, they gave up and sat on the floor to play with the boys.

When the kitchen timer sounded, and Otis didn't respond, Caroline found him and Dan in the mancave, deep in conversation. Unable to hear what they were saying, she knew by their intensity it was serious and left them alone. *Please let it be positive,* she thought, retracing her steps.

"Okay, Emmy, it's you and me in the kitchen to start the side dishes."

Her friend tied on an apron and grabbed a knife. "But you can't cook," she teased.

"Maybe not, but I can slice and dice."

"Just be sure to leave your fingers out of the recipe," Emmy said and was rewarded with Caroline's middle digit.

An hour later, Otis came flying upstairs, panicked by the time. Seeing his wife in the kitchen did nothing to relieve his angst. "Emmy, you let her cook?"

Caroline made a face at him. "I can prep, and you're welcome." With a sheepish grin, Otis thanked her and promptly threw them out of the kitchen.

Caroline went to freshen up before everyone arrived and found Dan in the library, holding the journal. "What a gift your mother left behind; what a beautiful soul she was," he said.

"Is," Caroline corrected.

Dan gave a sad smile. "Is," he agreed. "I guess I do need help. After reading the passages about my mom, I see too many likenesses, a pattern of behavior I don't want to continue to follow. As you said, Mom's situation deepened the black hole, but I no longer believe it was the cause." He stood and reverently handed the book to Caroline. "Thank you for sharing the pieces of your mother's heart." He kissed her cheek and turned to leave.

"Wait, have you told Emmy?"

"Not yet. We haven't had a private moment since my, um, enlightenment."

"Have one now; take a walk and talk to her. It will be the greatest Christmas gift you two ever received."

Dan gave her a bear hug and a compliment she cherished. "Like mother, like daughter," he said and went to find his wife. *So honored to be on your team, Mom.* Caroline set the journal down, gave it a pat, and went to welcome her guests with a much lighter heart.

★　★　★

Exhausted but content, Caroline lay in bed and recapped the day. All her Addisen Christmases were special, but none more so than today's. The joy Teddy and Caleb shared at the wonder of Santa and Christmas morning was something Caroline hoped to make a tradition. The spark of hope and love reignited in Emmy's eyes when she and Dan returned from their walk, and the bliss Dolcie's delight sprinkled over the day with her two families together. How the children loved Papa Bert the same and accepted his transition as only pure hearts can. The non-stop laughter and chatter as people from different walks of life bonded over great food and holiday spirit. *Yes, this was a perfect day, one for the ages,* Caroline thought. "Otis, are you awake," she whispered.

"Uh-huh."

"Whatever advice you gave Dan this morning in the man-cave worked; he's going for help."

Otis was quiet for so long that Caroline thought he'd fallen asleep. "I wasn't the one giving advice. He was," he finally said.

That was not the day's end I expected or wanted. Unwilling to cloud the day, Caroline let it be. But the comment was enough to gray her thoughts and chill her warm feelings. Less content than before, she closed her eyes and tried to sleep.

After the holiday hoorah was over, and everyone returned home, Caroline asked Otis about the conversation. His reply startled her. "I don't ask what you and Emmy discuss. Why don't you afford me the same privacy?"

Her ego bruised, she replied, "Fair enough, have it your way. I just thought it might eliminate some of the stress between us." *Two steps forward, one step back.*

Frustrated and hurt, Caroline turned her thoughts to the fast-approaching spring. She was concerned the corporate accounts would strain Cardinal's young supply, but Emmy assured her the nursery could handle it. The foreman promised to have recruits for her to interview in February, leaving plenty of time to train. She reviewed the numbers again, and even with the bank note, they worked, but barely. The inevitable snafus would be challenging, but Caroline was confident she'd find solutions. With everything ready, Caroline silently promised to spend the next weeks focused on quality time with Teddy, Otis, and their marriage. She knew once the season opened, it would consume much of her time and energy and put added strain on a relationship already weighed down. Once again, she wondered why it was so difficult, then remembered a Barack Obama quote: "Change is never easy, but always possible." *Let's hope he's right.*

I can't believe it's Valentine's Day! The last six weeks have flown by, full of family time and fun. Otis joined Teddy and me on some of our walks, and we'd hike to the ridge and light a fire to roast hotdogs atop our winter wonderland. I took a picture of Teddy and Charlie, their backs to the camera, as they sat and looked out over the ridge, with the fire in the foreground. Teddy's hand rests on his dog's back, and Charlie leans on him in devotion. It captures the very essence of unconditional love and friendship. I want to have a painting done to hang over the fireplace.

We've watched movies, played games, baked cookies, and gone skating as a family. There were plenty of snuggles, storytelling, and crafts made. What hasn't happened is a discussion between Otis and me on how to handle what is around the corner. The week after next, I go to Boston for weeklong interviews, the start of Cardinal's season. Spring and summer are Otis's peak times, and without a plan, disaster is guaranteed. As much as I hate to break the fairytale spell we are under, it's time to return to the real world. I will initiate a conversation tomorrow. Ugh.

Chapter XXXII

"My Boston trip is soon, and shortly after, all hell breaks loose for both of us."

"And?"

"We need a plan, Otis."

"Not really."

Here we go again. Otis felt her go still and turned to face her. "Caroline, how do we plan for chaos? The unforeseeable, the unexpected? We can't. As a team, we just need to commit to successfully figure it out as it happens."

"And if we can't find a quick fix? What then?" Caroline shook her head. "We need to be organized, prepare for the worst."

"The worst? Now who's setting us up to fail?" Disappointed, he left the room.

★   ★   ★

"How is having a plan a bad thing?" Caroline was pacing the Cardinal office, venting to Emmy.

"It's not when possible. But I agree, it's not realistic in this situation; there are too many variables. Besides, Otis knows our tribe will make it work. He did say he's on your team and committed to success. Did you register that? Seems like a corner turned to me."

Crap. "No, I did not. I was too focused on being organized."

"Organized, or in control?" Emmy let that sink in for a minute. "You're not in the advertising world, and Otis isn't your competition, Caroline. Maybe you need to exorcise your professional mindset of villains and vampires."

Caroline grabbed her coat. "Sometimes you really piss me off."

"I know. Usually, when I'm right."

"I'm going for a walk."

"I figured." Emmy smiled as her friend stormed out the door.

Caroline took a couple of deep cleansing breaths and let nature work on the cobwebs tangled in her psyche. Her vision tunneled on the adjustments expected of Otis, she had not made any adaptations of her own. Caroline now admitted she did see Otis as competition, not as a threat to steal business but to prevent success. Was it the same thing? Did it matter if it was? *No, and yes, nitwit. One is intentional, and the other might be a figment of my imagination. That difference lays the adjustment at my feet, not his.* She also needed to fully listen to what Otis said before forming a response. *I was busy preparing a comeback and missed the significant shift in his perspective. A committed team: precisely what I asked of him. Emmy's right; it's a control issue, mine. I can't expect his support in this undertaking without an equal say.* Caroline headed back to the office, more self-aware, less indignant, and a little humbled.

"How's Dan doing?" Caroline asked over lunch.

"He's made progress, but it's slow going. He goes to talk therapy once a week, and that's helped, but they haven't found the right combo of meds yet. It's a lengthy process."

"And you and Caleb?"

"Much better. I found a support group that helps me understand the disease and offers advice on explaining it to Caleb. It's a blessing to know you're not alone and your fears and frustrations are valid."

"Do you have any residue animosity?"

"No. I was furious at Dan's refusal to admit the problem. I saw it as a betrayal to us, his family. I have a better grasp on what he was — is — going through and realize my anger was misplaced. We now approach this as partners; we will fight and eventually win together."

"It sounds like you're going to war."

"We are. Like Dan told Otis on Christmas, marriage is an alliance of two, pledged to conquer any enemy, be it another person, illness, career, change, disaster, grief, or anything. They only succeed if they work towards an end goal as one. If the enemy is allowed to infiltrate and divide, the marriage will fail." *So that's the advice Otis was talking about.*

"That's such a male analogy. But it got through to Otis where I could not."

"It got through to both of them, so kudos to the metaphor." The friends clinked their teacups in a toast. "Maybe we need to start thinking more like a man," Emmy snickered.

"When pigs fly."

"Well, there was that cow that jumped over the moon..."

★   ★   ★

February became spring that turned into June. Life moved at a fast and furious pace, with plenty of obstacles along the way. But as Otis predicted, everyone pitched in and maneuvered around them, usually no worse for the wear. Until an unexpected, devastating blow brought everyone to their knees.

Otis's phone rang at 3:00am, never a good sign. Caroline

heard Otis say he'd be right there and asked him if Teddy, sleeping at Emmy's, wanted to come home. "No, that was Bert's night nurse," he said, pulling on his sweatpants.

"I'm coming with you." *This can't be good*, she thought, rushing to dress. They were at Dolcie's cabin within five minutes. The nurse met them outside, tearstains on her cheeks. She had gone to check Bert's vitals and found him cradled in Dolcie's arms. Dolcie waved her off, said there was no need, and insisted the woman give them privacy. That was an hour ago, and Dolcie still wouldn't let her in. Otis calmed the nurse and called the paramedics while Caroline quietly entered the bedroom.

"Dolcie," she said softly. "You have to let him go."

"I did. I held my husband until he found the light like I promised. Here, peacefully in his bed, held in the arms of the woman who's loved him for over fifty years. I didn't want him to take his last breath surrounded by strangers, noise, and fluorescent lights." Dolcie heard the rescue's siren and, with a ragged breath, kissed her husband for the final time. "Goodnight, dear," she said and went into the bathroom, where sobs of grief and heartbreak wracked her body.

That was the only breakdown Dolcie allowed herself over Bert's passing. Despite the attempted brave front, sorrow and loss cloaked her in a melancholy she could not hide. Still, Dolcie insisted anything more would be a pity party for herself, and she needed to stay strong for her family.

There was a lovely lakeside service, after which people were invited to share an anecdote about Bert. A celebration of life was held at Otis and Caroline's, with Bert's ashes set in a place of honor, surrounded by pictures and mementos. Late in the afternoon, Dolcie pulled Caroline aside and asked if she'd take her home. "My sons can take it from here," she said. "My graciousness is depleted."

Dolcie sat quietly on the ride, her arms wrapped around her husband's urn. *She looks so fragile, so lost...* Once home, Dolcie asked Caroline to make tea and went to change. Worried at how long she was gone, Caroline found her in a robe perched on the edge of the bed, silent tears streaming down her face as she stared at the urn on the dresser. "I can't seem to stop crying." Caroline knelt in front of her and held her shaking hands to comfort her. "How will I know he's okay? He'll worry about me alone and allow himself no peace; I know he will."

"Bert will see that you're fine and have peace," Caroline stated firmly. "I promise." She led her out to the porch and poured the tea. As the two rocked silently, a young cardinal landed in front of Dolcie. Caroline watched as belief ignited a light in Dolcie's heart and eased her pain.

"Well, I'll be damned," she said hoarsely.

Chapter XXXIII

Dolcie left with her family to spend time with each son and heal. She asked Otis and Caroline to keep Bert at their place so he wouldn't be alone and promised to be back and ready for her boys on the first of August. She was saddened to miss Teddy's birthday until he promised to have a second one when she got back. It was the first time they heard her laugh since Bert died.

Dolcie's departure at the height of everyone's season seemed insurmountable, but teamwork prevailed once again. Otis spoke to the camp manager and asked if they could spare a counselor for the rest of June; he could not but did have openings for preschool day camp. Immediate problem solved. Caroline crossed her fingers and called Will, hoping he and Hector could split July. "Sis, there's no way we can take time away right now, but I have an idea. Let me make a call and get back to you."

The phone rang and finally ended the longest afternoon of her life. "Well?" Will told her Miguel was going through a bad breakup and mentioned he needed a timeout. He was thrilled at the prospect of a month in Addisen, hanging out with Teddy and Caleb. "*Yessss!* Will, you're a bloody genius, and I love you," Caroline said.

"Oh, I'm a genius now, am I?"

"Temporarily," she teased.

Will chuckled. "I'll take it. Just glad I could help." Caroline hung up, remembering all the times he'd helped, fixed, or advised her through life. *I would be lost without him; he adds so much to my world.* She went to tell Otis the good news.

With the major crises behind them, everyday hiccups seemed easier to manage. The extended heavy rain in Boston that delayed projects, Dan's all-night trip to pick up a nursery order needed ASAP, and the rental cabin fire where luckily no one was hurt, all doable in comparison to the loss of Bert, and Dolcie's hiatus.

There was another loss, albeit smaller, that occurred. At camp, Teddy excitedly talked about the upcoming Fourth of July events, and an older camper informed him that the hoopla was about the country's birthday, not his. Crushed, he came home, and his parents assured him the celebration was for both, but his naivete and ego had suffered a blow. The incident triggered Otis's want of another baby and reminded Caroline the agreement was to revisit the idea in a year. The couple set a date night for the weekend to allow time for each to collect their thoughts. *Lessons learned.*

★   ★   ★

On Thursday, Caroline and Teddy set off on their morning walk. Caroline's intuition urged her to go a different path, and she trusted the instinct. The pair began to hear a low drumbeat echo through the trees. As they drew closer, Caroline felt its hypnotic vibration penetrate her body and beat as a second heart. She noticed that her son, and the critters, were also affected. They neared a small clearing and heard a deep, reverent voice melodiously chant in tandem with the drum. A lone man sat in the pine needles, his eyes closed, and swayed to the rhythm of his prayer. He was a big, solid man with leathery skin and long hair. His mystical presence and lined face portrayed someone on in years, but his physical bearing and jet-black hair were a contradiction.

Enchanted, mother and son stood in silence until he finished. He sensed their presence, opened his eyes, and with a sweep of his hand, invited them to join him. Before Caroline could respond, Teddy plopped down, nearly in the man's lap, and introduced them. "Hi, my name's Teddy, and that's my mom. What's your name?"

"Awasos," the man replied, unfolding his large frame to stand until Caroline was seated.

He saw the perplexed look on Teddy's face and clarified. "It's Wabanaki for Bear."

"My dad calls me Bear 'cause I'm a Teddy. We have the same name, sorta. What's a Wa- Wa...?"

"Wabanaki," the man finished with a smile. "It is the Native American confederation my nation, Penobscot, is a part of."

"Huh?"

Awasos explained. "Five tribes got together and formed a group to work as one. We call the group Wabanaki."

"Oh, like Caleb and me have a no-girls-allowed club. Wait—a tribe? You're a real Indian? Why aren't you dressed like one?"

As Caroline went to remind her son of his manners, Awasos quieted her with a twinkle in his eye. "I assure you I am, young man. We only wear traditional garb for ancestral rituals and celebrations now."

Caroline answered her son's question before he asked. "Special occasions, sweetie."

Teddy looked at him in total awe. "Are you a chief? Is that why you have that cool drum?"

"No, little Bear, I'm a shaman."

"What's that?"

"A healer."

"Like a doctor?"

"Ahhhh..." Before he continued, Awasos glanced at Caroline, who nodded her consent. He tried to describe it in a way Teddy, young and unfamiliar with his culture, would understand. "I heal people's minds, bodies, and spirits by guiding them through prayer and song. We believe we are one with nature and revere, greatly respect, its wonder and power. We sing to honor all its life forms and express our gratitude for what it brings to us. We celebrate its wholeness within us. You came upon me singing such a song: *Earth my body, water my blood, air my breath, and fire my spirit.* We sing in prayer. Do you understand so far, my friend?"

"I think so," Teddy replied.

"As a shaman, I was granted an extraordinary gift. Through prayer and meditation, I can connect the natural and spiritual worlds."

Confused, Teddy shook his head. "There are two worlds?"

Awasos nodded. "The earthly world we walk upon, and the world we rise to when our present time ends."

"You see and talk to dead people?"

"People do not die, young friend, only their vessel, the body. Their essence, the soul, lives on and ascends to the spiritual realm. From there, they help protect and guide us. Sometimes they come to us as a vision or in animal form. I am a chosen one, honored with the ability to call upon, see, and hear spirit, to bring their messages and wisdom when needed. This is what my people believe."

Caroline and Awasos exchanged an understanding gaze, then she looked at her son, "As do I," she said. The shaman nodded.

Captivated, Teddy wanted to pray as an Indian. Awasos placed the drum in Teddy's lap and taught him the words. As she listened to her son chanting, Caroline was struck by a sensation so intense it brought her to her feet. Awasos walked to her and looked knowingly into her eyes. He placed Caroline's hands, one on her chest and one on her stomach. "You have received a message. Listen to your heart and follow your core. Only then will your decision be true."

"Thank you," she whispered.

He spread his arms, looked to the sky, and smiled. "Thank them; I am merely a conduit."

On their walk home, Caroline saw the cardinal and gave thanks again.

"Mom, why did you talk to that bird?"

Distracted, Caroline answered, "It's your grandmother."

"Oh. Like Awasos talked about." Caroline was relieved she didn't have to explain.

Chapter XXXIV

Late that afternoon, a small drum arrived, dressed in beads and feathers. The accompanying note simply read, "Be well, young bear, for you are watched over. Your friend, Awasos." Otis was surprised when he heard of their morning adventure. Years had passed since the Penobscot nation lived on the mountain. Teddy related every detail. On his way outside to drum for Charlie, he remembered one last thing. "Oh, and Dad? Grandma has feathers now." Caroline laughed at her husband's expression and explained what had happened. Otis speculated the confederation had a conference in Portland, which brought Awasos to the area. Caroline knew better but chose to share only with her journal.

Such a spiritual experience! And to have Teddy involved was phenomenal. I have zero doubt Awasos was guided to us, sent to explain, and demonstrate the spiritual connection to Teddy, to teach him the art of prayer in its most natural state. And to send me a message I could not ignore or misconstrue. When my son started to drum and pray, I was consumed by a montage

of feelings so intense and powerful I reacted as if a bolt of lightning had penetrated my mind, body, and soul. It brought me to these enlightening thoughts:

Relationships are living, breathing things. An offspring, if you will, of the people involved. Like us, they must be nurtured, open to change, and willing to grow to thrive. Like a child, they must be well-tended to remain healthy, stay strong, and maintain the optimal bond. Marriage, friendship, family kinship, or parenthood, all connections need fairness, respect, and compromise. Because the good of the whole is what ultimately makes individuals happiest.

I've learned much this past year: I no longer view compromise as self-sacrifice, nor a difference of opinion, or suggestion as criticism. I try hard to fully listen before devising a response, and I heed advice from those I trust, even when it angers me. Partnerships of any kind require equal voice, and being prepared doesn't always mean a plan. Teamwork can handle any disaster, and it's impossible to love all of someone all the time; be it a spouse, friend, sibling, or yourself. (Charlie and Teddy are exempt). Lastly, I need to work on boundaries, mine, and others.

Would I have concluded all these things without that fateful morning epiphany? Eventually. But not in time for date night. Once again, the gift of spirit was present, guided me, and gave me clarity. I am blessed.

On Saturday, Miguel announced that he and the boys were camping that night, which scared the wits out of everyone. A city slicker in the Maine woods with two young boys could not happen. When Otis said as much, Miguel doubled over in laughter. "Good God, the woods? At night? We'd need a grown-up for that. I'm talking lights out, cooking hot dogs and beans in the fireplace, toasted marshmallows for dessert, and sleeping bags on the floor. Of the cabin."

"And no bedtime," the boys chorused, jumping around.

"And no bedtime," Miguel promised. He collected the boys, Charlie, and all the 'camping gear' and gave the two couples a wink on the way out. "If I were you, I'd turn in as soon as we leave."

Dan and Emmy headed home for their date night, and Otis surprised Caroline with an invitation to a candlelit picnic on Teddy's ridge. Otis set up tiki torches and prepared wood for a small fire while Caroline spread the blanket and food. Chilled lobster with a touch of lemon and dill, jumbo shrimp with homemade cocktail sauce, French bread, assorted cheeses, and a yellow beet salad with pine nuts. It was a meal fit for royalty. "What, no dessert?" she teased.

Otis opened a sack and pulled out the makings for s'mores. "Addisen's delectable treat of summer," he said with a bow.

Caroline gave her hair a flirty flip and looked up through her lashes. "Are you attempting to woo me with delicacies and charm?"

"Guilty as charged, milady."

They looked back over the year as they ate, all the shifts life had taken, and adjustments made. They each confided the inner turmoil they'd gone through and admitted the loneliness they'd felt, even in anger.

"So, what have we learned? Ladies first."

Caroline shared her journal musings and looked to Otis.

"Well said, and I concur. But I have a couple to add: communicate, even when it's ugly. Things got clearer once we started the mancave dialogues." He related Dan's analogy and the impact it had on him. "I realized we weren't functioning as a united front but as opposing sides. And lastly, a solid marriage requires complete trust in your spouse, which sometimes takes blind faith to accomplish."

Caroline kissed him softly. "Insights I hadn't thought of," she said.

"So, are we ready for a baby?" he asked.

They talked about the foreseeable future and what it would entail. Dolcie was on in age. Would a baby be too much? They decided no. The boys loved summer day camp if needed and would start school in September. Caroline wanted to expand Cardinal to Cape Cod, Rhode Island, and Connecticut, considerably extending her workload and travel. What if she hired someone from that area? She could manage the company's growth and stay in Addisen to raise their family. It would gratify the whole of her. "Sounds like we have a plan," Caroline said.

"An outline," Otis corrected.

"I stand corrected. Want to get started on making a baby?"

"Ya gotta love delicacies and charm," he mumbled, easing her down on the blanket.

★   ★   ★

Dolcie returned on the first of August, looking more rested but still short on sparkle. She assured everyone that all that was needed was her own bed, time with Teddy and Caleb, and the view from her front porch. Otis picked her up for a time, but soon, Dolcie insisted on riding her bike. They were encouraged by the show of spunk; could sparkle be far behind?

One late fall morning, a bicycle bell announced her arrival, and the boys ran to greet her as usual. Their whoops of joy sent Caroline and Emmy to the deck in time to see each boy lift a ball of fur from her basket. "Can we keep them? Please!"

"Absolutely not. The kittens are mine. But I did want you all to meet, and I need help naming them."

"I think you should name this one Teddy," Caleb said, and held his up.

Teddy pointed to the fur ball he was holding, "And this one, Caleb." Dolcie rolled her eyes. "Can't you two be a little more creative?"

"Are they girls or boys?"

She shrugged. "Don't know, but it doesn't matter. They'll come to eat when called, whatever their name."

Caroline and Emmy exchanged a cheerful glance. *Dolcie was on her way back.* While the boys played with the kittens, Caroline asked where she'd gotten them. "I was having coffee on the porch Saturday, thinking how lonely it gets without Bert. My cardinal landed on the hanging plant and sat there to keep me company. I thanked him but mentioned I needed a little more sometimes. Suddenly, I heard soft mewing come from under the porch and found these two without a mama. I took them in for the weekend, it worked out for all, so we decided to be roommates." It was not lost on Caroline that Dolcie had called the bird her cardinal and therefore knew Bert had brought the kittens. *Though heaven forbid, she ever admits it to anyone.* Caroline saw the twinkle in Dolcie's eye and knew it didn't matter if she shared. Her heart believed, and her sparkle had returned.

Epilogue

Caroline sat in the rocker, her baby girl at her breast. She loved to nurse, surrounded by her mother's energy. Perfectly content with Meri-Rose nestled close and Charlie at her feet, Caroline closed her eyes and replayed the last eighteen months like a movie in the theater of her mind.

She conjured up the tenderhearted elation she and Otis shared as they viewed the positive pregnancy test and saw the joy and wonder on their son's face at the news.

Caroline's stomach flipped as she recalled her panic at the realization her third trimester and birth would be at the height of Cardinal's season. And felt again the cleansing relief when all was resolved. Tired of the café, Hector had asked to market and manage the new territory, "I want my mojo back," he stated. Caroline loved the idea; they were an unstoppable team at PG&G, but what about the boards he sat on for Otis? Otis offered to split them, which added to his load but made it all possible. *Compromise, teamwork.*

With his meds regulated, and therapy, Dan was his old self again, and he and Emmy were ready to have a baby. *Quite the leap from Emmy prepared to leave, and Dan teetering on the edge of an abyss. Proof that treading lightly isn't always the best footfall; sometimes, you need to trample the brush and tackle the beast (issue) to bring it down.*

Meredith Rose Addisen, named after her grandmothers, was born July 26, two weeks early. Teddy is convinced it's because she wanted the same birthday month as her big brother. He dotes on her constantly, and Caroline is reminded of her childhood with Will, confident her son and daughter will share the same bond. *Will. Always present, always there for me.* The difference is he now asks for her guidance and advice as well. Evidence that relationships can transform without drastic change, such as role reversal. *It's all in the attitude and how it is perceived.*

Meri-Rose's arrival eased Dolcie and Charlie through the heartbreak of Teddy and Caleb starting school. Each getting on in years, they use the lull in activity to prepare for the burst of nonstop energy that races off the afternoon school bus. Dolcie loves the uninterrupted time to coo to and rock the baby, and Charlie lazes happily with her two cats, Spot and Rover. The afternoon returns to the familiar whirlwind of action, just as dear to her heart, with Charlie rested and ready to romp after two growing boys. "It's the best of both worlds," Dolcie likes to say.

Miguel returned to the city last fall but still spends much time in Addisen. He started painting again (something he enjoyed in his youth) and is inspired by the raw, naked beauty of Dame Addisen in the winter months. Miguel has an uncanny ability to see the soul of whatever he paints and captures it on canvas. *Our friend is really quite good,* Caroline thought. *I should have him paint the print* of *Teddy and Charlie on the ridge.* She thought of the comfort and wisdom her mother's words had provided to so many: herself, Dan, Emmy, Will, and in extension, Otis, Hector, Teddy, and Caleb. The heart of Addisen.

Inspired, Caroline gently placed her sleeping daughter in the crib and reached for her journal as a cardinal landed on the sill to say good morning to her daughter and granddaughter.

About the Author

Belle A. DeCosta's memoir, *Echoes in the Mirror*, was published in June 2020, and her piece, "An Introduction", is featured in the 2020 ARIA Anthology, *Hope*. Her novel, *Treading Water*, published November 2021, was awarded Finalist for Best First Novel by Next Generations Indie Book Awards 2022. Her piece, "Favorite Neighbor", is featured in the 2022 ARIA Anthology. Iconic Rhode Island.

Belle has had a lifetime of involvement in dance and choreography. She is the creator and director of Tap N Time, a seated tap and rhythm class designed for the elderly. Previously, she owned Belle's School of Dance for 25 years, and was founder and director of VERVE Dance Co.

When not traveling to nursing homes to share her program, she enjoys spending time with her grandson, being in nature, dining with friends, and, of course, writing.

Belle makes her home in East Providence, RI with her coonhound Trista and an aquarium of assorted fish.

She is a proud member of ARIA—Association of Rhode Island Authors.

Visit her at http://www.belledecosta.com.

Made in the USA
Middletown, DE
24 October 2024

62748280R00096